THE
OTHER
SIDE
OF
LOST

THE OTHER SIDE OF LOST

JESSI KIRBY

HARPER TEEN

An Imprint of HarperCollinsPublishers

Library of Congress Control Number: 2017959284
ISBN 978-0-06-242424-2

18 19 20 21 22   PC/LSCH   10 9 8 7 6 5 4 3 2 1

First Edition

For Sabrina

Anyhow we never know where we must go
nor what guides we are to get—men, storms, guardian angels . . .
—John Muir

TWIN STARS

WE LIE ON our backs on the trampoline, drawn into the center by each other's weight. The universe stretches wide above us, framed by a ring of mountains. My cousin and me at its center.

Twin stars, as our moms always say.

They smile and laugh and get teary-eyed together when they tell the story. Every birthday, before the candles and the wishes. How their due dates were weeks away from each other, but I was late and Bri showed up early, like we'd made a pact to enter the world together. And just a few hours apart, we did.

Tonight, we are thirteen. A number that feels like balancing on the edge of who we've always been and everything we might become. Here, now, there is only one thing I know for certain: that we'll figure it out together, no matter what directions life takes us in. I look at my cousin, my own true north, and I can't imagine it any other way. In the pale light of the stars, she reaches a hand up to the sky like she might pluck one from its place.

"Look up," she whispers, "or you'll miss it."

"Miss what?" I ask. I bring my eyes to the sky, and a tiny white light streaks through the darkness.

I blink, and it's gone.

"That," she says. "An extra wish."

She takes my hand. "We get to make this one for us, together," she says, "so I wish for us to always have adventures, and explore, and do all the things other people think we can't, and be brave, and free, and happy."

I laugh. "That's a lot of extra wishes."

"It's our birthday, we're allowed." I can hear the smile in her voice. "Your turn."

I look at the sky above us, and I think of today, with its special kind of birthday magic. My mom and me, rising before the sun to make the drive from the beach to the mountains. The crisp smell of the air when we arrived. The way Bri and I crashed into each other for a hug after being apart too long. A day's adventure with our moms—the hike to a rushing waterfall, a picnic lunch on sun-warmed rocks.

The four of us, holding hands as we made the jump into the clear, icy lake.

And later, dancing in the kitchen while our moms cooked dinner and laughed over stories of when they were young. Homemade cake, served on the front porch so we could blow out our candles just as the stars began to shine. The small, wrapped box containing the dreamcatcher keychain Bri had given me to match hers.

And this feeling. Lying beneath a limitless sky, and knowing I am exactly where I belong.

It's hard to imagine anything better than this, right now.

"I wish for us to always be like this," I say finally.

Bri squeezes my hand. "Of course we will."

LIKE THIS

I HEAR MY mom talking in the kitchen. "I'm coming," she says firmly. "That's it. You can't be alone today, not like this."

In the hallway, I stop midstep. I know by her words and the tremor in her voice that it's my aunt on the other end of the line.

I watch her reflection in the living room window, pacing the kitchen as she cradles the phone between her ear and shoulder. "No, I mean it. I'm coming right now. I'll get Mari up, and we'll get on the road right away. We'll be there in a few hours, like—"

She stops, and I see her take in a breath. I finish her sentence in my head: *like we used to.*

But she doesn't say it. Because it hasn't been like that for a long time.

I take a step backward to slip away to the safety of my room before she can see me.

"Yes. I'll tell her. Don't worry about that right now, it'll be here when we get back." There's a pause. "I love you too," my mom says before she hangs up. And then she just stands there, perfectly still, in the middle of the kitchen.

The low buzz of the refrigerator grows louder in the silence that follows. I don't dare move. In the window, I watch my mom's reflection. Her chin drops to her chest, and her shoulders begin to shake. She brings a hand to her mouth to stifle the sob that comes next. A lump rises in my throat, and all I can do is slip back down the hall, disappearing beneath the sound of grief that I don't know how to share.

I am eighteen today. Bri should be too.

I pretend to be asleep when I hear footsteps in the hall. My mom pretends to be okay when she opens the door.

"Mari?" she says softly. Her voice is still thin, like it might break any second. I hear her cross the room, and then the edge of the bed dips as she sits down next to where I lie with my back to her. She puts a hand on my shoulder.

"Good morning, sweet girl."

I feel a twinge of guilt at the old nickname, and I give in.

Open my eyes. Turn to my mom.

She smiles a close-lipped smile, and her eyes blink back tears that I don't want to see fall.

"Happy birthday," she whispers.

I don't say anything.

We both know that it's not.

She takes her hand from my shoulder and folds it into her lap, then she presses her lips together and takes a deep breath, and I know what's coming.

"I think we should go to Aunt Erin's today," she says.

I want to close my eyes again. Pull my covers over my head and disappear.

My mom reaches for my hand. "I just was on the phone with her, and she's . . ." She shakes her head and sweeps a finger beneath her eye. Sniffs. "Today is so hard, and I don't want her to be alone." She wraps her arms around me and pulls me into a hug that is tight and uncomfortable. "Come with me?" she asks softly. "I know she'd love to see you."

I pull away.

"I know this must be hard for you too, baby, but maybe it would be better if we were all together?"

I shake my head. "No," I say, "I can't."

"Why not?" my mom asks softly.

Because I will only be a reminder to my aunt of what she's lost. Because I can't go and act like Bri and I were still close, and things hadn't changed between us. But most of all, because I can't imagine being there, at that house, without her.

"Because I have plans," I say. "With Ian."

A half-truth.

My mom frowns. "Can't you reschedule? I'm sure he'd understand."

"No," I say. "He's planned some big surprise—for my birthday."

A flat-out lie.

It puts my mom in a difficult position, just like I know it will, and I try to ignore the pang of guilt I feel. Because I can see that she's weighing her sister's grief against her daughter's wish to avoid it. It's a losing battle.

"I *really* don't want to leave you alone on your birthday," she says after a long moment. "Especially this one."

"I won't be alone."

"But I may be gone for a few days, depending on how she's doing."

"I'll be fine."

She looks worried as she reaches out and tucks a strand of hair behind my ear. "I just don't . . . How are you dealing with this? With Bri. I've been so busy, and you have been too, and I don't even . . . I don't know if you're okay." Tears, again. "Are you okay, Mari?"

Her concern makes a tiny crack in me, one I can't allow. I take her hand in mine. "I'm okay, I promise. Go see Aunt Erin. She needs you."

She bites her lip. "Are you sure you'll be all right?"

"Yes."

"I'm so sorry," she whispers.

"Don't be sorry," I say softly. "But please tell Aunt Erin that I am."

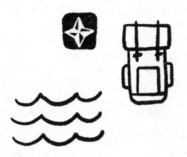

ALONE TODAY

I STAND IN the driveway in my pajamas and wave as my mom pulls away and drives slowly down the street. Even when I can no longer see her, I stay there, picturing each of the turns that will eventually take her to the long highway that leads to my aunt's cabin in the meadow.

And all I can think is that I should've gone with her.

I should be in her car, heading north to do the hard thing and go be with my aunt today because Bri no longer is.

I look down at the phone in my hand and I know that if I called my mom and asked her to turn around and come back, she would. I imagine telling her that I don't want to be alone today either, and that I want to go with her, and I want to be strong enough to be there for Aunt Erin. But I could never say those things. I'm not strong enough for any of them.

I'm weak. And hollow. And I can't think about it anymore.

I stare at my phone screen a moment longer, wanting a distraction from the knot of guilt in my stomach, and there are plenty at my fingertips. I tap the Instagram icon and get ready to see how many new likes and comments have come in since I last checked my Last-Day-As-A-Seventeen-Year-Old post yesterday. It takes a second to refresh, which makes me both hopeful and anxious, but then the little bubble appears and shows me my numbers at a glance:

Likes: 1,423

Comments: 112

New Followers: 47

Which brings my total number of followers to 582,419. Not terrible, but not as much as I'd hoped for with that post. I'd ridden my bike down to the beach just before sunset and set up the tripod, then held my hair above my head and waded out into the cold water up to my chest so that my skin would shine wet in the golden light. It had taken so many attempts with the wireless remote, and then even more edits when I got home, but the end product was a shot of me in the sunset, looking out to the ocean like I was looking out at my future, tanned body on full display in a bikini I would never actually wear to the beach.

I read the first comment, from **@BohoFit81** Beautiful soul, and an inspiration to all of us!

My eyes trace the outline of my waist, where I'd used an app to take just a touch off each side, and then the "empty" beach, which I'd created using another app to erase unwanted things in the background—in this case, people. And of course there's the light and color of the shot, which I'd manually edited for a more subtle effect than the standard filters. I feel a twinge of shame at the effort that went into the effortless-looking shot, but I answer her anyway:

@BohoFit81 Thank you so much! But it's all of you beautiful souls who inspire me!

I add the smiley face with the kissy heart emoji and hit Reply. Then I look up and realize I'm still standing in my empty driveway, and that if I want to get my first post of the day up in time to be there when people reach for the phones on their nightstands, or while they have their first cup of coffee, I need to hurry.

#BREAKFASTGOALS

IN THE KITCHEN, I arrange a rainbow of berries and nuts over a bowl of oats dotted with chia seeds. Once I've got it just so, I drizzle a thin line of agave syrup as artfully as I can over it all, then finish with a small purple orchid I pluck from the plant on the counter. Next, I clear off a space on the granite for the walnut cutting board I use as a background for food shots, and set the handmade bowl on top of it. I have to climb onto the stool and stand above the counter to get it centered in the frame, and when I do, I can see it needs something more. It is, after all, my birthday breakfast.

I pick the last of the flowers from the orchid and spread them around the bowl, hoping it looks like a celebration. It takes only a few shots to get the angle and perspective right, then I sit right there on the counter and get to work with the photo settings to find the right mix of light and color. Once I do, I add my caption and tags: Birthday breakfast of choice. Good food = a good mood. #birthdaybreakfast #whatieatinaday #foodshouldbebeautiful #veganrecipes #plantstrong

Finally, I double-check it all, push it out to my other accounts, and hit Post. And then I wait for the first few likes to come in. It's only a moment before they do, and once they hit double digits, I climb down and dump the bowl into the sink, ignoring the empty gnawing in my stomach. There is no way to shave inches off my waist for video, which is what the next post needs to be, so food can wait.

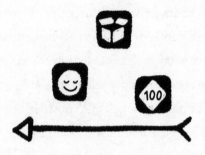

#FITSPIRATION

UPSTAIRS, I TEXT Ian to see if he'd be willing to meet me for lunch somewhere, then I dig through my closet for the yoga pants and bra that I'm supposed to do a paid post for. After I find and put them on, I stand in front of my full-length mirror and examine my reflection. The first thing I see is a hint of roundness in my stomach. I suck it in and pull my shoulders back, trying to lengthen my frame and practice looking natural at the same time, which only sort of works. At least the bright blue and turquoise of the outfit pop against my tan skin, and the top is padded, which gives my tiny boobs some much-needed help. My hair hangs loose and wavy over them, and though it bothers me to have it down during actual yoga poses, it looks better that way, so I leave it.

I open the laptop on my desk and switch over to the video camera that's permanently pointed at the one clean corner of my room—my "yoga studio." A bright mandala tapestry hangs against the white wall. Below it is a mat laid out flat on the hardwood floor, and framed by a set of artificial tropical palms. I step onto the mat and look into the camera, conscious of the blinking light that means it's recording. After a few deep breaths, I shake out my arms and look, for a long moment, into the lens. Then I begin to move and breathe through the series of poses I've been practicing, working up to a difficult handstand at the end. My body feels weak and tired, but I try to focus on looking at ease and fully engaged in each movement and moment.

I'm not, though. Thoughts of Bri and my aunt and my mom creep into my mind and throw me off balance so that I have to start over, again and again. Too many times to count. By the time I finally make it all the way through to the handstand, my heart is pounding in my chest, and my arms are shaking so badly that I want to scrap the video altogether. But that's not an option, because I'm already behind on posting for this company, and I promised a peak time slot in my feed. I have to work with what I've got.

I sit down at the desk and check my phone for a reply

from Ian—which there isn't—then tap over to my feed to check on my breakfast post. The numbers are still steadily climbing, which is a good sign I got it right, as basic as that post might have been. I scroll through the comments, liking them all as I go. They're mostly happy birthdays and emojis—heart eyes, smiley faces, the yummy smile. A few people have actually written the words *yum* or *yummy*. A follower named **@peace_love_plants**, who likes and comments on everything I ever post, wrote: Looks delish! HBD, beautiful!

Thank you so much! I type. And then I roll my eyes and put my phone down.

I sit there in the silence of my room, which feels emptier knowing my mom is likely making her way through the desert by now. It'll be a few more hours until she reaches the mountains, but I picture her arrival. I know she and my aunt will wrap their arms around each other and cry together right there in the driveway before they go into the house. Maybe after a little while, they'll decide to go for a walk or a hike somewhere and talk about how it used to be. They'll sit on the deck and watch the sun sink behind the mountains. Maybe they'll even lie on the trampoline and look up at the stars. No matter what, they'll be together today.

For a moment, I let myself imagine being there with them. But when I start to tear up, I force my eyes back to the computer screen and get to work editing a half hour's worth of yoga footage down to the best forty-five seconds I can find, making sure to include the handstand at the end. I watch it back a few times, and am surprised at how much better it looks than it felt. Satisfied, I caption and tag it:

> Dreamy morning flow to celebrate another trip around the sun.
> Full of gratitude, today and every day, for what is still to come.
> Bra and pants from @spiritual_luna all-new summer line!

I grab my phone and go over to my bed to take a break, but the sun shines in through the blinds, too bright where I lie. It shouldn't upset me, but it does. I get up and yank the string to close them, and my curtains too, then I sit on the floor in the dark and the glow of my phone.

I glance down at it and see that my video is up to seventy-eight views already, but Ian still hasn't texted me back, so I message him again, despite the fact that it makes me feel slightly pathetic: Hey! Let's meet today for lunch—my treat—and a few quick shots for that lifestyle account.

Just as I hit Send, a comment notification pops up. I tap over to it, hoping it's more than just an emoji.

@soulmagic Why are you so fake? You're missing the entire point of a yoga practice. Don't act like it's a spiritual thing for you—just come out and say you're trying to show off your ASSets and sell us something at the same time. And then eat something, for fucksake.

Another comment appears before I can answer, this one from **@wildchel326:**

@soulmagic Seriously? Mari comes from an authentic place every day, with every post. She chooses to share her life with us, so you need to lay off. Just because she mentions a product she likes and wears DOESN'T mean she's trying to sell us on it. And what exactly is wrong with being fit and healthy? Go pour your hate elsewhere. Namaste.

I stare at the words, written in defense of me and my sincerity, and it turns my stomach the slightest bit. It takes a moment, but I type what I hope sounds like a genuine response.

@wildchel326 Thank you for being the positive energy that keeps me going. Amen, and namaste for beautiful vibes.

I finish it off with the prayer hands then hit Reply.

I'd like it to be true—that positive comments like hers are enough to insulate me from the negative ones, but it doesn't work like that. Especially not when the negative comments have some truth to them that even I recognize.

My phone buzzes with a text from Ian:

Yeah, but can't stay long

That's fine. Usual place?

Sure

When can you meet?

5

Okay. See you there.

He doesn't bother to answer, let alone wish me a happy birthday, even though I know he's probably seen my posts. But we look like a happy couple on each of our feeds, which is beneficial to both of us, especially for companies looking to capture crossover accounts—and for a while now, that has been enough. At least that's what I tell myself.

#COMBINEDREACH

AT 5:45, Ian steps out onto the back patio of the vegan café we use as our favorite, looking put out. He looks even more annoyed when he sits down and I take the birthday gift I'd wrapped myself out of my purse.

"Really?" he asks, eyeing it.

I ignore the sting of his coldness. It wasn't always like this. "Really," I say softly. "It's my birthday. So it can be your gift to me, and it covers all bases."

We're both quiet for a moment, then he nods like that makes sense. "Happy birthday then," he says. "Works for me." He picks up his fork to dig into the plate of food I ordered that has long-since grown cold.

I reach out a hand to stop him. *"Wait."*

He rolls his eyes and puts his fork down. "Jesus, Mari."

I flag down the passing bus girl. "Excuse me? Would you mind taking a few pictures for us?"

"Of course!" she says with a wry smile. "Are they gonna end up on your feed?" The prospect seems to make her night.

I smile back. "Maaayybee."

I hand her my phone, then put the wrapped gift in the middle, between our plates. Ian's hand reaches for mine across the table, and I take it. We look at each other and smile like we're enjoying dinner and each other's company.

"Aw, that's so cute," the bus girl says. "I'm gonna take a lot so I make sure to get you a good one. You guys smile, just like that." She backs up another step, and I hope it's enough to get the whole thing in the frame.

"Open it," Ian says in a voice that sounds like he genuinely wants me to. Like what's in the box came straight from his heart.

"Yeah!" the bus girl agrees. "I'll get a few of that too!"

I smile, like together, they've convinced me, then I tear the handmade paper I bought on the way over. She snaps away as I open the box and take out the necklace I knew would look perfect with the low-cut dress and push-up bra I'm wearing.

"It's so beautiful," I say, dangling it in front of me and looking at Ian as lovingly as I can.

"Here," he says, standing. "Let me."

He takes the necklace from my hand and steps behind me, smiling in that relaxed way he does so expertly. I lift my hair and dip my chin, and smile in that diminutive way that I do so expertly.

"THAT is adorable," the bus girl says.

And I know we have the shot. A perfect candid.

Ian knows it too—I can tell by the way he starts fidgeting as soon as she stops taking pictures and hands my phone back.

"That necklace is so pretty! And you guys are SO cute. Hope I got you some good ones."

"I'm sure you did," I say. "Thank you so much! Want me to tag you, or credit you?"

"Really? Of course! I'm Kayleigh Bee," she says, and I search for her name. "It's k–a–y–l–e–i–g–h–b, all lowercase."

I type it in. "Is this you?" I hold out my phone for her to check.

"Yep. That's me. I follow both of you guys, so this is kind of—sorry, fangirling just a little."

"Well, thanks again," Ian says. I hope she can't hear the edge of irritation in his voice.

"Anytime, seriously."

The sound of glass breaking interrupts what is about to stretch out into an awkward moment. Kayleigh glances over her shoulder. "I uh . . . I better get that. See you guys next time?"

"Hope so," I say. "Thank you."

As soon as she turns around, Ian takes a breath and lets it out in a loud sigh. "We good? Cuz I gotta go."

I nod. "Yeah, sure. I'll get it up tonight."

"Great," he says. "Make sure you tag me."

"Of course."

"Happy birthday, Mari."

"Yeah."

He turns to go before I can say anything else.

I gather my stuff and leave some cash on the table before anyone can notice.

#MAKEAWISH

THE HOUSE IS dark when I get home, and I walk straight through to the backyard, not wanting to feel the emptiness of being inside alone. Outside, I set the mini cake, sparkler candles, and lighter on the table and turn on the pool lights. I don't bother with the patio light. The soft aqua glow and the candles should give off enough light for this last shot.

I sink into the patio chair, completely drained. People are going crazy over the shot of Ian putting my birthday necklace on me, oohing and aahing over how cute we are, and how sweet he is, and how beautiful the necklace is, and wanting to know where they can get it.

It makes me want to throw my phone in the pool, but I put it down on the table instead and get the cake I bought on the way home out of its box. It's too small for eighteen candles, so I settle on a triangle of three in the center of the cake and then grab my phone and try a few different angles that will include me blowing them out with the pool as the background. This one's going to be hard, because it can't look like a selfie. That would be mortifying.

But it so obviously is with every angle I try. I dig the mini tripod and remote out of my purse and get the frame set up so that my cake and I are backlit by the pool, both of my hands seemingly free. I sit there for a moment, staring at myself on the phone screen. I look as worn on the outside as I feel on the inside. My hair falls in soft waves over my shoulders, and the makeup I put on before dinner is still perfectly intact. But the effect of them can't hide the flat look in my eyes, or the hint of dark circles beneath them— or my cheeks, which look too hollow in this light. None of it can hide the emptiness I feel in this moment.

I light the candles. Click my remote as I blow them out. I do this again and again, as many times as it takes to get the shot right.

I don't bother to make a wish.

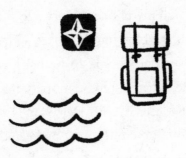

SOMETHING TRUE

UP IN MY ROOM, I watch my phone screen, my pulse ticking off the likes as they roll in. I try to feel the little lift they used to send through me, but tonight it's long gone. Now I just watch with anxious expectation. There's a pause, a break in the flow, and I feel the familiar tug of self-doubt. The heaviness of it starts to sink me lower than I already feel. I wait a moment. Wonder if I chose the right shots, if I posted too many. If I should just take them all down. I hold my breath, at the edge of tears, which I know is ridiculous, but I can't help it. After what feels like forever, I see the little notification heart, and then another, and I breathe again. There are comments coming in too, and I scroll through the ones on my birthday wish photo. Sprinkled in with the celebratory emojis are a few actual comments:

> HBD Beautiful!
>
> My birthday wish is to be YOU.
>
> BIRTHDAY GOALS
>
> Hope all your wishes come true, forever and always.
>
> OMG LUV U SOOOO MUCH!!!!!!
>
> You are amazing and beautiful and OMG, if we ever met, I know we'd be INSTANT BFFS.
>
> Make a wish! Perfect end to a perfect birthday!

They're all so sweet, and I know I should go through and make sure to like each comment so they know I've seen and read them, but something in me rebels at the thought. I lie back on my pillows, close my eyes, and think about these strangers—my followers—and how they think of me, and feel like they know me because of what I show them. They have no idea that I am sitting here by myself in my room on my birthday, and that it is the loneliest thing I've ever felt.

My phone pings with an unfamiliar notification, and I tap it without thinking. Immediately, my stomach drops, and I wish I could undo it.

> Erin Young tagged you in a post with Bri Young!

I stare at their names in shock. I've spent the entire day doing everything I can to *not* think about Bri.

And now she's right in front of me.

I stare at the notification about my aunt's post until the letters blur and float in front of me, then I do something I haven't done in forever. Not even in the two months since Bri died.

I click over to her Facebook page.

The cover photo takes my breath away even though I've seen it before.

Bri stands atop a granite ridge surrounded by blue sky. Her eyes are closed, and her face is turned upward toward the sun. She reaches her arms up, open and wide as her hair swirls around her in the wind, long strands blowing over her smiling face. It's the one my aunt chose for the memorial program, and I can see why. Whoever took it somehow captured her whole spirit in one shot.

Directly beneath it is my aunt's post. It's the picture of us from our thirteenth birthday. My throat tightens when I look at the image. Bri and I stand side by side, arms intertwined, grinning and holding our matching dreamcatcher keychains proudly in front of us.

My aunt's caption reads: Happy Birthday, our twin stars. Keep shining your beautiful lights for this world to see.

The words land in the center of my chest. I want to send them away, to close the page and act like I never saw it.

But below Aunt Erin's post are more words, more birthday wishes for Bri, and I can't help but read those too.

> Happy 18th birthday, my friend. I think of you every day. I feel you in the wind and see you in all things beautiful. Love and miss you every day.

> Thinking of you today and your adventurous, free-spirited, humble, and kindhearted way. I promise you I will try my best to live life to the fullest, just as you did, to honor you and our memories. Love you always. Happy birthday, Bri.

> So many tears today. I miss you and your sweet smile, your beautiful voice, and your powerful spirit.

> You had a wild heart and a gypsy soul, and I know you're out there somewhere, exploring the great beyond and shining your light down on all of us. Happy birthday, beautiful angel.

They continue on like this, as far as I can scroll down, these heartbreaking birthday wishes for my cousin, from people I know and don't. Each one strikes a chord somewhere deep in my chest, and my own tears begin to fall as I read them.

Tonight, I don't have the strength to fight it.

I think of us, and how we used to be. Of that last birthday

we celebrated together—our thirteenth—when the possibilities for everything we could be were bright and endless. And together, we were invincible. We could do whatever we wanted, and the two of us together were enough. That's how she made it feel.

I think now, of the wish I made on that birthday—that it would always be like that with us.

It was so long ago. Before I screwed everything up.

Before my dad left, and my mom got so wrapped up in making a new life for herself that she forgot I was still trying to figure out how to live mine. So I looked elsewhere for help, and I found it online. First, it was a girl on Instagram who posted pretty pictures and inspirational thoughts, and I clung to them and the escape they offered me. And then I started to find more accounts like hers, of all these girls, living out these perfect, inspiring lives that I wanted so much. They were beautiful, and happy. They spent their days eating healthy, and doing yoga, and going to the beach with their friends.

So I watched these strangers' lives from a distance, and it didn't take long for my envy to turn into emulation. I studied their poses and posts, memorized quotes and hashtags, read articles on how to build a following. I went through my own account and deleted the photos with the fewest likes, and the ones that didn't fit in with the overall image I wanted to create—that of a blissful, balanced life. A life that was better than the one I was actually living. This image couldn't include shots of me in my Halloween costume as a ten-year-old—or filthy and sunburnt after a day of adventures on my thirteenth birthday with my cousin. I felt guilty about taking that one down, but I did it anyway. And when Bri noticed and asked me about it, I lied and told her how sad I was that those posts had somehow gotten lost. She sent me the pictures again, but I never put them back up.

Instead, I composed pictures I thought more people would like. Other people, who didn't actually know me. And when I posted my first bikini shot, it worked. Almost overnight, strangers started liking my posts, and commenting, and following me. Bri had messaged me asking what was going on, and if everything was okay, like she could see right through me—which I hated. That first picture, and the response it had gotten, had made me feel good when nothing else did. And I didn't want her to take that away from me.

So I posted more like the bikini picture, and every single one widened the distance between us. I didn't want to hear her question me, or be worried, or call me out on something false I said or showed. She knew the real me, and that was not the one I wanted everyone else to know. So I'd stopped calling her. Made excuses not to visit. It's hard to face someone who can see the real you, so I didn't. I let her go. And eventually, she did the same with me.

A lump rises in my throat, and Bri's Facebook page goes blurry through my tears, and all I want is for her to be here right now. To celebrate our birthday together. To talk to her. To pour out the loneliness of my days.

And to confess the meaninglessness of the life I've created for myself.

Maybe that's what makes me get up from my bed and sit down at my desk, in front of my laptop and hit record.

My image comes up on the screen, and I sit there in my pajamas, face streaked with mascara, eyes puffy and red. And for once, I don't care. I stare at the unblinking eye of the lens, not knowing what to say. And then I picture Bri on the other side, listening. I think of us, and of the summer of thirteen. The last time I saw her.

"It's our birthday today," I say. "And there's something I need to tell you." I pause. Stare at the lens again. And finally, for the first time in forever, I say something true.

THE LIFE I CREATED

BEFORE I EVEN open my eyes, I have a bad feeling. In my mind, I can hear my tear-choked voice, and see my face on the computer screen, and I will it to have somehow been a nightmare, or something that I only imagined doing, then thought better of. But even as I reach for my phone, I know I'm wrong. I stare with sleep-heavy eyes at the thumbnail image of my teary face. And then the number beneath it. The one that has happened, literally, overnight.

784,062 views

A record for me.

I think I might throw up.

My god.

I hit the play button, and when I hear the tremor in my

voice, I feel like I can't breathe.

I watch myself look right into the camera and decide to bare my soul to my cousin. I tell her it's our birthday, and then I let loose the flood of everything I'd been holding back, every toxic, painful thought.

I cringe at my words and the pain in my voice when I speak them, but it had been a relief to say these things out loud—that my life feels empty and meaningless. That I want to quit it all. The pictures, the videos, the constant worrying about followers and likes and numbers. The fakeness of all the paid posts, and the loneliness of spending every moment making my life look like it's perfect and like I have it all when really I am miserable.

I say them out loud, all these things that have made me so hollow inside.

I tell her how I've completely lost myself to them. How I have given my days to creating a fake life to convince other people of what? That I'm worthy? Admirable? Enough?

I tell her that, on our eighteenth birthday, I am none of those things, and that I have no idea who I am or what's even real anymore.

And then I tell her how I wish I could go back to when we were thirteen, and I did know—because of her. Because she was always so sure of who we were, and what our lives would be.

I bring up how at the memorial, my aunt talked about

the way Bri had lived the seventeenth year of her life like she somehow knew it would be her last. And how as she spoke, a slideshow played behind her—of Bri's last year. She'd spent most of it backpacking her way across Europe after graduating early. There were shots of her riding a moped through the Italian countryside, standing on the top of a mountain in Switzerland, living with a group of hippies on a beach in Tenerife, then coming home only to hitchhike her way up to Canada, where she danced in ice caves and found frozen waterfalls nestled in snowy mountains.

I talk about how after that had come pictures of Bri training to hike the John Muir Trail for her eighteenth birthday. Our eighteenth birthday. I'd forgotten all about that plan of ours, but she hadn't. She hadn't forgotten about any of the plans we'd made lying on the trampoline in her meadow that last summer. Plans for all these things we were going to do together someday.

Things that she'd actually gone out and done.

I tell her I wish I'd been with her. That I wish I'd never gotten so sucked into my stupid fake life that I stopped living a real one. I tell her I'm sorry. So sorry. That maybe if I hadn't completely lost myself, I would've been with her on all these adventures.

Or on that hike.

That maybe then she wouldn't have taken that one wrong step. And maybe my aunt wouldn't have had to get up in front of hundreds of people at the memorial and tell them that Bri had felt no pain when she fell. That she'd just been out on the trail, living the life she loved one moment, and gone the next.

I tell her I don't love my life at all. But I want to start. I want so badly to do something that is real. That means something. I want to feel a connection—to life, and the world, and to other people.

I want to feel something besides self-loathing.

At the end of it, when I run out of tears and confessions, I promise her I will. I will change. I will do something different. It's then that I look directly into the camera and say with great resolve: "This is why I'm quitting social media. To stop living in a screen and start living an actual life."

And then I'd posted it on my YouTube channel.

The irony of this is not lost on me.

But I'd wanted to do something to make it more real. Maybe to hold myself to my promise. To give my words weight.

So I'd put it out there, for anyone to see.

And now seven hundred and eighty thousand people have.

Notifications ping continuously from all of my social media accounts. Texts roll in from numbers I don't recognize.

The views tick up and up.

I am paralyzed. Unable to stop the deluge happening right in front of me. Terrified to see what people are going to say.

But I have to know. I have to see what they're saying. I take a deep breath and scroll down through the comments:

Holy shit, girl. Dropping some truth.

This made me cry. I'm 20yrs old and literally everything she said hit me hard.

So wait a second . . . you're gonna USE social media to QUIT social media???

My heart goes out to you for the loss of your cousin. Good luck with your new life! I hope you find happiness.

I can't anymore with these stupid white girl 1st world problems. Seriously, you're complaining about your life "looking" too perfect? You need to step out of your tiny fucking bubble.

Thanks for showing your insights, Mari. You're inspiring to so many of us. Keep your head up!

How do none of you see that she's just doing this for attention? This girl is a total fake.

Even her "boyfriend" is fake. Did you see what he just posted?

This is why I don't put my personal shit online.

Please. Go live your life where none of us have to hear from you ever again, you stupid bitch. No one cares about you or your cousin or your fake ass life.

Get a fucking life, hypocrite. Or better yet, take your own.

I stop reading. Contemplate the option for a moment.

I honestly don't know what other choices I have right now.

I can't take it back. Even with the positive comments mixed in, I wish, so hard, that I could undo that one click that put my most private, vulnerable thoughts out there for anyone to see.

But I know I can't.

Even if I took the video down, it's already been mirrored and posted all over the place. Memes of me crying into the camera already exist. Links have already been posted to a few online news stories with varying headlines: Instagram Star Quits, Saying Social Media Is Not "Real Life"; Insta-famous Teen Exits the Internet in a Teary Confessional—But Not Before Posting a Viral Video.

The links go on, as do the comments about them. There are even death threats.

This can't be real. It feels like I'm watching my life from a distance, speeding ahead, completely out of control, and I can't do anything to stop it. I don't understand why this is happening. I don't know why so many people care, or have an opinion about it, or me, and feelings I never should've shared. Why they feel like they can say all these horrible things. I don't know why *I* care so much that they do. Most of them are complete strangers, taking shots at me from behind the safety of their screens. But some of them . . . Some of them are people I know in real life. People who I went to school with, who are happy to have one more reason to hate me. Even Ian has joined the mob. His post this morning is a screen grab of me, puffy-eyed, red-faced, midsob with the caption that reads:

How's this for real? Glad this shit's over.

It already has over five thousand likes and hundreds of comments with people saying even worse things about me than they did on my video. No one calls him out for being a part of it. They save the blame for me, and offer to take my place at the same time.

I want to stay in the cocoon of my own bed and not come out until this nightmare is over, but I can't just sit here and let it keep happening.

I get my laptop and take the video down first. And then my YouTube channel. Then I move on to my Instagram account—thousands of pictures and videos that I poured years of my life into. I wipe them out with one click and then another. Paid posts that made me money and earned me free products—I delete them, and the chance that any of those companies will do business with me ever again. This is my one swipe at Ian. We were a package deal on many of these because of our combined popularity.

Once everything is gone, I close my eyes, take a breath, and let it out as slowly as I can, trying to figure out what to do next.

On the bed, my phone chimes with a text. I open one eye to see who it's from.

My mom.

I sit there a moment, frozen.

Until right this moment, I didn't realize that my mom seeing that video would be a million times worse than any stranger seeing it. I didn't even think about the possibility. She checks up on my social media accounts from time to time, lets me know if she thinks an outfit might be too much, but for the most part, she tries to trust me and let me have a certain level of independence with my online life.

But this video is different. It's more than I've ever told her—more than I'd ever want her to know, but it's too late now.

I take a breath, reach for the phone, and tap the message bubble to read her text:

Good morning, sweet girl! I hope you had a good day yesterday.
I tried to call, but reception is still terrible up here. Aunt Erin
is doing better today, and we're going to hike to the falls this
morning, so I'll be here for one more night as long as you're okay
down there. Sound good?

I exhale and thank the mountains around my aunt's house for the bad service that apparently hasn't gotten any better since I've been there. I type back:

Sounds good. Glad to hear Aunt Erin is doing better. I'm fine
here. Spending my first day as an adult lounging by the pool,
haha.

I add the laughing-crying emoji, then hit the arrow to Send, and watch the bubble as she types her response.

Hmm . . . not sure that qualifies as adulting, but enjoy it while you
still can! I'll call tomorrow when I'm on the road. Love you.

Love you too.

I set the phone back down on the bed and breathe a sigh of relief. At least this gives me enough time to try to do some damage control and figure out what to say to her when she gets home and we actually have to talk face-to-face.

I lie back on my bed and stare up at the ceiling. Regret hangs heavy and invisible over me as I replay my words, meant for my cousin, twisted by other people and quoted back to me over memes of me sobbing about my life and how pathetic it is. Words that came from my heart and felt true when I said them, but seem trite now. Cheapened by other people's opinions of them.

I hate that I put this part of myself out there for anyone to hear and comment on. But a piece of me feels a tiny measure of relief too. I wanted to cut ties with everything that felt false. Really, I wanted an escape from the life I created for myself.

But now that I'm free, I don't know what comes next.

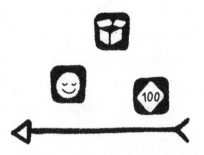

WHAT LIVING LOOKS LIKE

IN THE KITCHEN, I make a smoothie. Normally, I would take so long to set up a photo of it and then get it posted, that it would melt and I would dump it down the sink.

Today I sit at the kitchen island and sip it.

Through the sliding glass door that opens to the backyard, I can see the sun shining down on our pool, complete with its palm tree reflections, and in my head, I compose the perfect bikini selfie. I think of different angles and poses that would showcase the best of me while still being somewhat original. To offset the idea that the post was only about my body in a bikini, I would try to find a good quote to use as a caption. Something that would sound like I was spending my first day of being eighteen contemplating life's big questions by the pool. All of that together would create the kind of picture sure to draw comments about what a great body and life I have, while highlighting how deeply spiritual I am at the same time. A perfectly balanced representation of my brand.

For a second, I crave that rush of adoration. The red hearts of approval, and the flattering comments. But then I remember how empty it all felt—especially now—in comparison with the things I read on Bri's page last night. I hadn't bothered looking at her Facebook page, or even her Insta feed for the last few years because I knew it would make me sad. And when she died, I couldn't do it then either. I was too afraid to see the life she'd been living before it happened.

But now, today, I want to.

I rinse my smoothie glass in the sink, then go back up to my room, where my laptop lies closed on my bed. When I sit down and open it, my first impulse is to check on what people are saying about me. I stop and remind myself that it's out of my control, and that the only thing that *isn't* is what I do now. So what I do is open up Bri's Facebook page, and begin scrolling.

I scroll down past all of the birthday wishes, through the many, many pictures of her memorial. I want to find *her*, and the things *she* was doing and posting about. But I am stopped before I can get there by all of the photos other people have posted of her, and the kind, beautiful things they have to say.

In one photo, she stands in her hiking gear next to another girl hiker. The post reads:

So heartbroken to hear this news. I met you on one of your training hikes for the JMT. I was exhausted and out of water, so you filled my bottle from your own, then turned around and hiked back with me until we reached the trailhead. I can't tell you how much that small kindness meant, then and now. I will always pay it forward, I promise you.

Another post, written in a different language, shows her standing next to a guy our age, somewhere in Europe, holding a cardboard sign. I hit translate:

A few months ago I gave you a ride to see your relatives. Right now I have never seen a girl so brave, cheerful, and full of energy like you! I want to remember you always with the smile you had on your face.

The next one is from a woman in Italy:

Dear Bri, you are so missed, but we will never forget the gifts you've left us with. You taught us what living looks like. And loving too. With the heart first, always.

I scroll and scroll, through posts of the mountains of California, all the way up to Canada, then to the European peaks and oceans and squares of foreign towns. I study every photo, read every post. And though the people and places are all so different, there are two things that remain the same in each shot—Bri's open, joyful smile, and the way she seems to have touched everyone she met in a meaningful, inspiring way.

I go backward in time, closer and closer to when Bri was still alive, now more curious than ever about what she herself had posted, and that's when I find the picture I know—of her, standing atop the mountain, arms raised high. Her last post.

Off the list. ✓

Goose bumps rise on my arms. I wonder how many other things were on her list.

The sound of the doorbell yanks me back to here, now. I look out my window in time to see the UPS driver get in his truck and pull away from the curb in front of our house. When it disappears down the street, and everything goes still again, I realize I've been sitting here with my computer for hours. I still have so much more to read and go back through, but I'm thirsty, and need to get up and move.

Downstairs, I fill a glass of water and grab an apple from the bowl on the counter. On my way back upstairs, I pass by the front door, then stop, remembering the UPS truck. I peer out the peephole in the door, but I don't see anything. Beyond the doorstep, the street is empty and the sky is blue and cloudless. Slowly, I open the door. And sitting there right in front of it is a very large box, addressed to me.

The return address puts a lump in my throat.

I stare down at my aunt's name, and the address that immediately conjures the image of her cabin in the Sierras, tucked in its ring of mountains, the meadow in front thick with tall grasses and wildflowers, the trampoline nestled within them.

Bri and me, lying there on our backs, watching the thunderheads build and gather on summer afternoons.

I sink down, right there on the front step that's warm from the sun, next to the box.

My birthday present.

Even after we stopped celebrating our birthdays together, my aunt Erin never forgot my birthday. Of course not, since it was Bri's too. Every year, a package would arrive from her. And every year it was something the old me would've liked, something I wasn't interested in anymore—a leather-bound blank journal, a set of paints and brushes, a book about the constellations. They were all whispers of things I'd loved in my childhood, things I'd long since outgrown, and they always went straight into the back of my closet where they were quickly forgotten.

I sit there next to the box that is much larger than anything she's sent before, scared of what it might contain. Certain that it will have something to do with Bri for this, what should've been our eighteenth birthday. I can't decide if I want there to be something of hers in this box or not.

I stare at it, like if I do long enough, I'll be able to see through it to what's inside and decide if I want to open it. Birds chirp from the surrounding trees. A car passes by on the street in front of the yard. A slight breeze carries the smell of fresh-cut grass and hint of the nearby beach. Life goes on all around me like it doesn't realize how badly I've screwed it up, or that Bri is gone, or that there are some things, like this box sitting on my front step, that are too much for a person to handle.

All of a sudden, I feel very tired. I close my eyes to shut it all out, but for the first time since I've stepped outside, I notice the warmth of the sun on my face. I breathe, in and out, I don't know how many times. Enough to take the edge off the panicky feeling in my chest. And when I open my eyes, the box sits there in the sunlight, waiting for me to do something.

It's awkward to carry, and much heavier than I expect it to be. I have to catch my breath after I get it into the living room. I grab a pair of scissors from the kitchen, and pause in front of the box. Then, with a deep breath, I slice through the packing tape and lift the flaps open, one by one.

Sitting on top of a layer of bubble wrap is an envelope with my name on it.

I swallow, and take another deep breath as I pick it up. I try to see through the translucent layers of plastic to what's beneath, but I don't remove them. Not yet. Aunt Erin wanted me to read this first, that much is obvious. I break the seal on the envelope, take the crisp white stationery out, and begin:

Dear Mari,

I hope this makes it to you in time for your birthday. I can hardly believe that you're going to be eighteen . . . time goes so fast. Too fast. I wish I could slow it down. Some days, I wish it could go in reverse. There are so many things I would change.

I know that you and Bri weren't close these last few years, and that's one of those things I would go back and try to change. Family is everything, and you two were even more than that. Your shared birthday was a shared piece of heart and soul. You were our twin stars.

Both of your lights still shine, so brightly. Bri's now, from a different place. I feel her shining her love everywhere—in the mountains and the sky, the sunrise and the evening breeze. Nature is where I go when I need to breathe. And nature is where I find her. But a few weeks ago, I was in her room, and I felt her more strongly than I have since she passed.

As you probably know, she was planning to hike the John Muir Trail this summer to celebrate her birthday—your birthday too. She'd spent months researching and planning and training for it. Every penny she earned went toward buying the equipment she was going to need for her trip.

I was sorting through it all, wondering what to do with it, when I knew—out of nowhere—that you should have these things. I know it sounds strange, but I am learning to trust these moments. I also know that your life is so different than Bri's was, but I want you to have these things, and I believe in my heart that she does too.

It makes sense to me, in a way that is very Bri.

You were never far from her thoughts. And though she was planning this as a solo hike, I know she never let go of the idea that you might join her—your name was on the wilderness permit months ago, when she applied.

Your life has taken you in such wonderful and exciting directions, and I have no doubt that there are big things in store for you and your future. Maybe one day that will include a journey like the one Bri had planned. I hope so. I love the thought of her things making their way over those many miles one day, even if she can't. I know she would love that, so it brings my heart peace to pass these things along to you on her behalf.

Happy birthday. We love you and are so proud of the beautiful young woman you have become.

Love always,

Aunt Erin

I sit there a moment, stunned. In total disbelief that after all these years and all that distance, Bri still thought of me. That she still put my name on the permit. That my aunt would send me her things, believing that I would ever deserve to have them.

I'm ashamed she thinks I do. She has no idea who I've become, and how small and empty my life is in comparison to what Bri's was. To what her life should *still* be. She was the one actually living. Finding herself and the world, while all this time, I've been losing those same things. And now it's too late. *She's* lost to me too.

I'm certain I don't deserve whatever is in this box. Her things. But my aunt sent them here, to me, and I can't just put them away like all of the other birthday gifts. I take a deep breath, then reach into the corner of the box and peel back the layer of bubble wrap. Sitting there, taking up all of the space in the box, is a moss-green backpack. But it's not like any backpack I've ever had. It's huge, and covered in zippers and compartments, clips and straps that look like they all serve a purpose. And pins and patches that don't. Attached to the topmost zipper is something I recognize.

It's her dreamcatcher keychain.

HER BOOTS

I STARE AT the small dreamcatcher with the sunflower at its center for a long moment, remembering how Bri had always had it on her daypack when we went adventuring, and how I'd watch it swing from side to side whenever I walked behind her. She'd gotten it from some gift shop somewhere near Yosemite, and I'd loved it so much when I saw it, she made Aunt Erin drive her all the way back to get me a matching one for my birthday. I haven't seen or thought about mine for years.

But Bri's is here, sitting right in front of me, on a back-pack that is almost the size we were last time we saw each other.

I try to lift it out, but it's packed full and is so heavy that

I have to stand and use both my arms and the strength of my legs to get it out of the box. I drop it on the floor and it lands with a thud, sitting upright on its own. I walk a slow, cautious circle around it, like it's a living, breathing thing.

Bri was going to carry this? For how many miles?

She was always strong, but still. I can't imagine. I kneel down in front of the pack, thinking that I should probably leave it as is—zipped up and ready to go. But curiosity gets the best of me, and I reach for the straps that hug it tight, wanting to know what my cousin put inside. One by one, I pinch the plastic clips that release the straps, and then I reach for the zipper of the top pocket.

Inside there are Ziploc bags, so many, and I pull them out one by one, examining their contents. There is a compass and Swiss Army knife. A small, thin book called *The John Muir Trail*. A lighter and matches that say they're waterproof. Two tiny bottles of something called Aquamira. A small headlamp and what looks like a homemade first aid kit with bandages, Neosporin, alcohol wipes. There are chargers, batteries, wires. A bag of protein bars and energy gels. A poncho. A Ziploc filled entirely with Advil. Another lighter.

And that's just the beginning. Everything is compact and meticulously packed.

I lay it all out on the carpet, and then I move on to the next compartment. Here, I find a large plastic canister containing more plastic bags of what looks like food and maybe toiletries, two water bottles and a clear vinyl bag with a spout, a mug with a spork that folds up attached to it. A contraption with a bottle and a tube that looks like some kind of filter. Something I'm not sure of—a tiny stove? Beneath all of that, there are utilitarian-looking clothes, a tightly rolled sleeping bag, and what must be a tent.

I keep going, taking each item out of the pack and examining it like the foreign object it is to me, impressed that Bri knew about all of these things and how to use them. By the time I lay it all out on the floor, it's hard to believe that it's everything she would've needed—and that somehow it all fit in that pack. Instantly, I wish I'd paid more attention to *how* it fit, because I can tell right now, I will never be able to get it back in.

I go grab the box to put it all in, and my breath catches.

In the bottom corner, a bit flattened from the weight of the backpack, sits a gray pair of hiking boots. I lift them gingerly and hold them with both hands in front of me. They're broken in, with dirt visible in the mesh over the toes, the turquoise of the laces dulled by a thin layer of dust. They're lighter than I expect, but the weight of them in my hands grounds me in the reality of what I'm holding.

These are her boots.

Who knows how many miles they've traveled, or places they've been? Who knows if they were the ones she was wearing when—I can't think about it.

When I bend to put them back in the box, I see there is one more thing inside of it. A manila envelope that lies flat on the very bottom. I pick it up then pinch the two wings of the clasp together so I can lift the flap. What I pull out is a leather-bound journal like the one my aunt once sent me. I open it. On the first page, my cousin wrote:

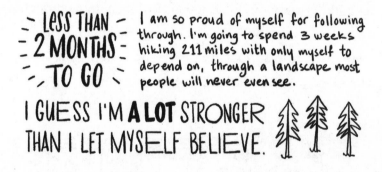

I run my fingertips over the curves of the letters that form these words, then down to the tiny mountain range she'd drawn at the bottom of the page.

I don't know how she ever doubted her strength, or her

courage. When we were kids, and I spent summers there in the Sierras with her, she was always the one to be brave. She was comfortable and in her element out in nature, whereas, being from the safety of suburban Orange County, I worried constantly about what might happen to us as I followed her up mountains with no trails and watched her climb trees so high she'd disappear into their branches. It was exciting and scary at the same time, but I always trusted that with her I'd be okay, and that she was sure of where we were going.

I turn the pages, and there are more entries. Some that look like notes about hikes, others that seem to be thoughts or quotes or maybe both. I flip past them, knowing I'll come back to read each and every one. And I hit a page titled Day 1, and a list that I realize is an itinerary:

☐ Pick up permit ↴
at Yosemite Valley
Wilderness Office
☐ BEGIN!
☐ First stop:
CLOUDS REST
10 mi, 9,931 ft

That's it for the first day. But every page beyond that is filled with a similar itinerary and a few notes. It's overwhelming to think about how much planning she had put into this trip, let alone what it would actually take to follow through with it.

But somehow she believed she could.

I flip back to the first day, and a shiver rolls through me when I see the date. It's two days after our birthday.

Tomorrow.

I look around at the equipment spread over the living room floor, her things that were supposed to travel the miles of that trail with her. Things she was going to carry, things that would help carry her.

And in the same way that she knew she would do it, I know I never could.

I wish I was the kind of person she was. Someone who would just go for it, no matter how crazy it seemed. And I am having a hard time ignoring the timing of her things arriving on my doorstep the day before she was supposed to start. But I have absolutely no business even entertaining the idea of doing something like what she was planning.

Just the thought of it scares the hell out of me.

I drop to my knees and frantically scoop the contents of the pack up in my arms, trying to stuff it all back inside. I shove Ziploc bags haphazardly into pockets, push the big things back into the main compartment, fight with the zippers and straps to close it all inside, where it belongs, but it's no use. It doesn't fit, no matter how many different ways I try. I step back to take a breather. The pack sits off-kilter for a brief moment, then falls over, spilling its contents back onto the living room floor.

I kick it. And then I sit down beside it and give up. "What am I supposed to do with this?" I ask the silence that follows.

There is no answer, no whisper of advice, no sudden clarity.

There is only me, and I feel ridiculous.

I leave it all there on the floor and walk away. Upstairs, to the quiet of my room, with her journal. When I sit down on my bed, Bri's page flashes back on to the screen where I left off.

I read the next post back:

> I decided a little while back to hitchhike from CA up to Canada to pay a visit to some friends (and make some new ones). The journey is almost done now, tomorrow will be my last day on the road! And I have a message to everyone who told me I was crazy—you were right, but hey, I still made it.

I shake my head, thinking of how when she did that, even my mom had wondered why my aunt had let her. And I remember thinking that the answer was easy. Even when we were little, there was no *letting* Bri do something. She did what she wanted. And I could only imagine that as she got older, and the world spread out wide and full of possibilities in front of her, that continued to be the case.

I look down at her journal in my hands, and open it to the second entry:

LIFE'S TOO SHORT to wake up in the same house every morning, see the same people every day, and follow a daily routine.

I only have so much time, and I won't waste a second. I want to see it all, I want to make a difference in people's lives, and I want

——TO BE HAPPY——

I look around at the room I wake up in every morning, with its drawn curtains and blank walls. The computer I've been living my life through. The emptiness that hangs over all of it. And then I reread the list of those things she wanted, things she was in the process of doing and being, and I wonder, for a moment, what that would feel like.

IN MOTION

I PACK QUICKLY so I can get on the road before I change my mind. It's tempting to stop and dismiss the idea because it seems so big and crazy. It would be easier to stay home and think it through longer. Plan. But I don't have time for that now. A quick Google search has informed me that Bri's permit needs to be picked up in person tomorrow morning in order to be valid, which means I need to leave this afternoon if I want to be there to do it.

I throw a pile of workout clothes into my overnight bag, along with a few basic toiletries, phone, charger, and earbuds. Then I stand in the middle of my room, looking around and trying to figure out what else I might need in order to do the first day of Bri's hike. I know how ridiculous it would be for me to even say I'm going to try anything more than that, which is why I haven't.

But I also know that my life can't remain as it is for even one more day. That *I* can't remain as I am. I knew it last night, and that's why I made that video. And today, I've been given a way to change it. For the first time in a long time, I feel like I have a chance to do something meaningful. Or at the very least, that I have a direction to move in.

I cross the room to my desk and pick up the program from Bri's memorial, with its picture of her standing on the top of Clouds Rest, arms wide open, like she wants to share it with anyone willing to go with her, and I tell her I'll go—at least that far.

Because it was my name she put on the permit. My doorstep her things landed on, after I asked for my life to change. It doesn't seem crazy when I think about it this way. When we were kids, she always knew right where she was going, and I followed wherever she went. And somehow, after so many years, and so much distance between us, maybe she knew that I would need to go. Maybe that's why she wanted me with her for this. So I have to go, even if she can't.

Especially because she can't.

I give the program one more look, then tear the picture off and slip it into my back pocket. Next, I grab her journal off my desk, and go downstairs to write my mom a note for when she gets home and finds that I am gone.

I know she'll freak out. And that she'll be upset with me for leaving like this. But I also hope that she'll understand that right now, this is something I need to do.

Mom,

By the time you get home today, I'll be on my way to Yosemite. I need to get away—you'll see why as soon as you're back on the Wi-Fi. But please, don't worry about me. I am okay.

Actually, I'm much better today than I have been for a long time. You probably know this already, but Aunt Erin sent me a birthday gift. It got here today and it's the backpack Bri was going to use to hike the John Muir Trail this summer— like we used to talk about doing together. She was supposed to start tomorrow, so I'm going to the trailhead—to pick up her permit, and pay my respects, and hike to the first place on her list.

I'll call when I get there. Please don't worry. I love you.

Heading north on the dusky highway at a steady seventy, I already feel like things are changing. I've never driven alone like this, far and fast, and there's a freedom in it that is quietly exhilarating. In the past, I've spent car rides with my head down, eyes on my phone, alternately scrolling and refreshing to pass the time without having to talk. A passive passenger. Now I'm the one driving. I'm the one deciding where I go. And I take it all in as I slice through the evening with the music turned up loud enough that I can't think too much about what I'm going to do when I get there.

For now, my destination is Yosemite Valley, where the John Muir Trail begins, and that's enough. I can't try to wrap my head around anything beyond getting away, like I'd told my mom. As I make my way through the central valley, I don't think about hiking. I just move forward. Far from my life and the mess I've made. I zip past fields and orchards of crops I can't name. Stinky farms with endless cattle. Signs about water rights everywhere. Billboards advertising Jesus as the one and only savior. I drive without stopping through towns with names like Pixley and McFarland, and farms dotting land so vast and flat that it's hard to believe that it'll ever give way to any mountains, let alone the peaks and domes of Yosemite.

I've seen photos of Yosemite all over Bri's pages, but never in real life. By the time she'd graduated to adventuring there, I'd graduated to amassing followers and perfecting lifestyle shots. But tonight, out on the road like this, away from everything, and beyond my comfort zone, I already feel distant from all of that. I glance down at my phone, and the red dot that is me making its way up the middle of California, and I feel the tiniest bit proud. I'm doing *something*. And to be in motion feels good.

Soon, the landscape begins to shift and change, and that feels good too. The valley gives way to rolling foothills, and the highway curves gently, weaving a wandering path between them. Every so often, another car will pass by, reminding me that I am not alone, but mostly, it's me and the road, and the black night outside.

After a while, the road begins to climb. The curves sharpen, and I take one a little too fast and have to fight to keep the car in the lane. I slow down after that. A sign warns to watch for deer, so I turn my brights on, hoping I don't see any shining eyes from the sides of the road. It grows steeper still, and now trees creep in from both sides, forming a tunnel that blocks out the sky. I don't know if I've ever been anywhere so dark.

The map on my phone says I'm not far from the entrance to Yosemite National Park, but that I'm still an hour and a half away from the valley floor, where the trail begins. I change my playlist to something upbeat and continue to push on at this new, slower pace, but it's not long before the reality of the previous sleepless night and the hours of being in the car alone start to catch up with me.

The initial adrenaline and excitement of taking off have faded, and I can feel weariness sneaking in. I pop a piece of gum in my mouth and roll down the windows all the way. Crisp, cool air rushes in, surprising for August. It carries with it the long-forgotten scents of pine and soil, of living things growing wild and green. I don't think I've smelled these smells in years, but immediately they bring back a rush of memories—a montage of summers spent with Bri at my aunt's cabin in the meadow. Sunrises watched from our sleeping bags on the trampoline, the freedom of days spent adventuring with a backpack and the sack lunches we'd pack ourselves, pretending like we were heading off on great treks into the wilderness. Nights spent dreaming up new adventures beneath a blanket made of stars. It feels like ages ago and like yesterday at the same time. My heart aches when I think about all of the lost time between then and now. Time we could've spent together, if things had been different.

I think of Aunt Erin's letter, and how she said she wished she could turn back the clock. God, I do too. I would change so many choices I've made and things I've done. Pulling away from Bri would be the first. For a second I let myself picture how different my life might have been if we'd stayed close. We would've celebrated yesterday together, I know that for sure. Maybe we'd even be in Yosemite already, sitting around a campfire, giddy with excitement about tomorrow. Over and over I'd be saying that I couldn't believe we were really going to do it, this thing we'd talked about years ago, when turning eighteen seemed like decades away and we had all the time in the world. She'd look at me in the warm glow of the fire and she'd smile that happy, radiant smile, and tell me she always knew we would.

In the distance ahead, I spot lights and the wide arc of a sign. As I get closer, the road widens into four lanes, each with its own kiosk beneath the sign that I can now read: Welcome to Yosemite National Park. For a moment, I almost can't believe I'm here. I slow the car and pull out my phone to take a picture, but then realize I have no one to share it with. Even the kiosk is empty when I pull up.

There are instructions on the window to continue in and pay on the way out if the kiosk is unstaffed. I sit beneath the entrance a moment longer. If I still had my account, and I posted a picture like this, the likes and comments would start rolling in immediately, even this late at night. Now is the time when people who can't sleep are still awake, scrolling away, envying other people's lives from a distance. That's what I did anyway, and I know I wasn't alone.

For a moment, I wonder what I'm missing, what all the other people whose lives I'm usually privy to are doing and posting. I wonder if any of them are still talking about me, or if I've already disappeared from their feeds and minds, like I wanted to. I don't know if I like that idea either, that it could be that easy to stop mattering.

After a long moment, I take a deep breath, put the car in drive, and try to just be here, where I am, doing my own thing. I realize as I pull forward that this is going to take some practice. Especially alone.

I roll down the road into the park, drained and all of a sudden unsure about being here. In the dark, it's not the majestic arrival I was picturing. There is nothing and no one to welcome or congratulate me for making it. There's just me and the night, and the exhaustion that grows heavier by the minute. I blink and widen my eyes to try to keep them focused on the road as it rounds curve after curve for miles.

Finally, I make it to a brightly lit tunnel, and I'm happy when I reach it. It's too long to hold my breath and make a wish like Bri and I used to do, but the lights are warm and bright, and somehow that makes me feel less lonely. But they don't make me feel less tired, so when I reach the end of it and see a small parking lot and a sign that says vista point off to the left, I pull off the road. My headlights cut through the darkness of the empty lot, and I park at the curb, facing a low rock wall and the darkness beyond. When I shut off the car and step out into the night to stretch, the absolute silence of the place is almost a sound in itself.

It's cold, and I shiver a little as I stretch my arms above my head. But when I lift my eyes to the sky, I forget about everything except what I see in this moment. Spread out in a vast, inky dome above me are millions of tiny pinpoints of light. It's not even a second before I see one streak across the night, leaving a thin trail of light behind it.

A lump forms in my throat, and my eyes water. Here is my welcome, and I know exactly where it came from.

"I made it," I say to the sky, and then I blow my cousin a kiss, and I make a wish.

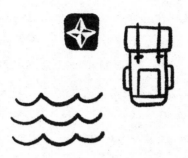

TO BE BETTER

A LOUD, INSISTENT tapping echoes in my head and rouses me more abruptly than I'm ready for. I'm cold and disoriented, trying to blink my eyes awake in the too-bright morning light. Facts rush in as I sit up and realize what's going on: I'm in Yosemite, slept in my car, and am probably about to get a ticket.

More tapping. The windows are fogged up so I can't see, but a voice, female and official-sounding, addresses me.

"Miss, I'm going to have to ask you to step out of the car."

"I . . . um . . . okay, just a sec." I look in the mirror, run my fingers through my hair like that will make a difference, and then glance around for my wallet.

"Miss? Please step out of the car. Now."

I open the door cautiously and do what I'm told. Standing there is not a police officer, like I was picturing, but a middle-aged woman with graying hair and glasses, dressed in head-to-toe green, complete with a ranger hat. I don't know why, but it puts me at ease to see her there. I smile.

She does not smile back. "There's no overnight camping in cars here in the park." She gestures at a sign just one space over. "It's clearly posted."

"Oh," I say. "I'm so sorry. I didn't see that. I got in late last night, and I was so tired I knew I wasn't going to make it all the way, so thought the safest thing to do would be to pull over and sleep."

She glances in the car. "You alone?"

"Yes, ma'am."

She nods. "It probably was the safest thing to do in your situation. But it's illegal here, and I'm going to have to write you up for it." She reaches for her ticket book then steps aside to speak something into her radio.

I gasp. Not at the fact that I'm about to get a ticket, but at what I see in front of me.

Where she stood just a second ago, a scene like a postcard opens up. The sunrise sky is the first thing I see. It's on fire with every imaginable shade of orange and pink and gold. I run my eyes over the landscape in front of it, in complete disbelief of what is spread out before me. It doesn't look like it could possibly be real.

Huge, towering mountains of rock jut out from the forest below, like they were thrust straight toward the sky by some massive, violent force. They stand like silent giants, cold and unyielding, except where the sunlight splashes them with its warm glow. In the distance, a waterfall spills down the face of a mountain in slow motion, and beyond that, Half Dome absorbs and reflects the deep orange light like a beacon over the valley.

I can hear the ranger talking, but I can't pull my eyes away. I've never seen anything so beautiful. I feel a tear slide down my cheek, and reach up to brush it away.

The ranger comes back over to where I'm standing. "You all right, miss?" she asks, her tone softer than before.

I nod, still unwilling to take my eyes away.

She stands beside me and surveys the valley below. "First time here?"

I nod again.

"It's a sight to see, the sun rising up over the land like that. Happens every day, but it never gets old."

I wipe another tear away. "No, I don't imagine it could, not here."

"Not anywhere," she says, her eyes scanning the sky. "Every new day is a fresh chance and a clean slate." She pauses. "You know what I mean?"

I nod.

"You headed down into the valley?"

"Yes."

"Passing through, or staying a while?"

I look at her now. "Passing through. Kind of. I'm starting a hike today."

She smiles. "Which one?"

I hesitate before I answer because I know that doing Bri's entire hike isn't in the realm of possibility for me. But standing here right now, with the sun spilling light over the new day, makes me wish it was. So I say it anyway.

"I'm hiking the John Muir Trail."

The ranger nods slowly. "Good for you, honey. I haven't done that one, but I know a lot of folks who have. That hike'll test you, truly, but it'll change your life."

"That's what I'm hoping for," I answer, surprised that she believes me.

She turns to me. "Well. You best get on your way. The Wilderness Office opens soon, and you'll want to get in line for your permit." She crumples up the ticket with my license plate filled in already.

"Really?" I ask. "Thank you. Thank you so much."

"Sure," she says with a smile that crinkles the corners of her eyes. "Everybody needs a break sometimes. Just make sure you pay it forward out there on the trail."

I smile. "I will. Promise."

I mean this when I say it. I'm so touched by the small kindness that she's just shown me, I want to be able to pass it on.

She nods and tips her hat. "Good luck. And don't forget, when things seem bad—and they will out there—every day is a chance to be better than you were the day before."

When I pull into the parking lot of the Wilderness Center, I try to remember this. The ranger's office doesn't open for another ten minutes, but there are already hikers lined up on the deck and gathered around the parking lot in small groups. They check gear and packs, cradle coffee in gloved hands, and talk and laugh in the cool morning air. They look comfortable, like they belong here. I try to tell myself that I do too, that this is my fresh start, but all I can think of as I get out of my car and take my place in line is that I'm in over my head.

A half hour later, when it's my turn to step up to the counter, the man there seems to agree. He checks my ID, and matches it with my name on the permit before he hands it to me. "And Bri Young?" he asks, looking over my shoulder.

"She's here," I say. "Outside. Watching our packs."

"It's just you two *girls*?" he asks, without bothering to hide his opinion about this.

"Yes."

"And your parents are letting you do this alone?"

"Yes."

"You see the movie, or something?"

"What movie?" I ask.

He raises his eyebrows in disapproval, then opens his mouth to say something else, but seems to think better of it. "Nevermind."

"Is that all? Can I go?"

"You girls need to be extremely careful," he says, instead of answering my question. "Especially with the winter we had. Rivers are the highest they've been in years. Crossings are treacherous. We've already had four hikers swept away, and lots have had to turn back on account of how much snow is still out there." He pauses a moment, and concern replaces his stern demeanor. "You're aware of all this?"

I am now. "Yes, sir," I say.

"And the bears are out, and they're hungry, so it's imperative that you stow anything and everything that could tempt them in your bear canister. Not just food. Toiletries too—deodorant, lip balm, lotion. Female products. Anything with a scent that might attract them."

"Yes, of course," I say, realizing what the plastic canister in my pack is for. I take a deep breath to try to calm the growing sense of fear in my stomach. I hadn't counted on having to contend with bears. "Anything else I should know?" I'm genuinely asking, and I think he sees it.

He glances over my shoulder at the line behind me then leans in like he's going to tell me a secret, and motions for me to do the same.

"Even experienced hikers don't make it the whole way. You're young and have plenty of time to do a hike like this. Just remember that. Nothing out there is worth dying for, so if you girls think, at any time, that you're getting in over your heads, there's no shame in leaving the trail, you understand?"

You girls.

A wave of nausea rolls through my stomach, and I almost tell him the truth—that my cousin was young and brave, and died training for this hike. That she was far more prepared and experienced than me, but I'm the one who's here now, alone, and I have no idea what I'm doing, or any business even attempting a tiny part of it.

I almost say to him that I don't know anything about crossing rivers or bear canisters, or how to work the stove in my pack. But I don't. I don't want him to try to talk me out of it, or tell me one more thing that I should be afraid of, because it might just be enough to make me quit before I've even tried. And then I'd be back to having nothing.

This, even if it's crazy, and foolish, and I don't have a chance at succeeding, it's something.

Right now, it's really the only thing.

"I understand," I say.

Apparently satisfied by my answer, he slides the permit across the counter to me. "Okay. Good luck, be safe, and don't forget to secure your food at all times."

"I won't," I say as I take the permit. "Thank you."

He nods in answer, and I turn and walk, permit in hand, past the line of hikers who all look more experienced and prepared than me. An older couple, decked out in matching cargo vests, cargo pants, and boots, look over at me as I pass. A young woman smiles then continues on with the conversation she's having with a man who looks like he's probably her dad. Last is a group of guys who look close to my age, standing in a circle in front of the doors I need to exit through.

"Excuse me," I say, just as they all burst out laughing at something. It's like I'm not there. I repeat myself, this time a little louder, with more confidence than I actually feel. "Excuse me."

One of them turns around and makes eye contact with me. His are a warm brown that matches his wavy hair, which is held back by a bandanna. "Sorry," he says. Then he turns back to his friends. "Hey. Move. She's trying to get through."

Still laughing, the other three guys step aside so I can pass.

I glance back at the one who made them move. "Thanks."

"Sure," he says with a dimpled grin. "See you out there."

I give him a quick smile but don't bother with an answer before I push through the door.

Outside, the sun is momentarily blinding, but the air still has a chill to it. I walk to my car then follow the directions to where the main parking lot and camp store are. The lot is already half full, and crowded with people standing around their cars unloading gear, bent over packs, checking equipment, and all generally looking like they know what they're doing.

I pull into the first empty spot I see and shut off the engine. Then I tell myself to get out and do the same, even if I'll be faking it. But I just sit there, watching through the windshield, trying to ignore the growing sense of fear from the words of the wilderness permit guy running through my head.

Four people swept away crossing rivers. Hungry bears. Snow in the middle of summer. Nothing out there worth dying for.

All of the reasons I shouldn't go speed through my mind, one after another. But then something else he said silences them: *You're young and have plenty of time.*

My breath hitches and a lump rises in the back of my throat.

It's what we all think—that we have plenty of time—but we don't know that for sure. Life can change in an instant. A single misstep on a familiar cliff trail changed Bri's. Any number of unexpected things could change mine. We don't see these things coming. We never plan on them happening, but they do—all the time, which is scary to think about.

I never thought about it before, but I know how true it is now.

There are so many things that could go wrong if I try this. I put my face in my hands and close my eyes and try to picture Bri here with me. Try to hear what she would say if she knew how afraid I was. It's quiet in the car, but through the open windows, I can hear the jovial voices of other hikers as they get ready, and beneath those voices, outside sounds—the distant rushing of water, birds chirping intermittently, a breeze moving through the tops of the trees. So much life, still going on all around, despite the fact that these things can happen.

Or maybe in the face of the fact that they can happen.

Maybe that's it. Maybe Bri was one of the people who knew that about life, and that's why she packed so much living into her days. Because they could be gone at any time, and she wanted them to count. She said herself she wouldn't waste a second, and she didn't.

I sit there in my car, on the valley floor of Yosemite, my cousin's backpack in my trunk, and her plans for the journey of a lifetime sitting on my front seat, and I want my days and my life to count too.

I want them to count for something more than what I've been doing, and I don't understand how or why I know, but this is it. This is how I start. Today. I start by opening the door, and letting the sunshine and the mountain air wash over me.

A MILE IN HER SHOES

BOTH KNEES ALMOST buckle and I struggle to stay upright under the immense, unwieldy weight of the pack. It bulges out in every direction, towers over my head, and tugs painfully downward on my shoulders, making it feel impossible to find my balance. Lean too far forward, and I'll end up face-first on the pavement. Too far the other way, and I'll be on my back, limbs in the air like an overturned bug, helpless and unable to get up. I take a deep breath and pull the chest and waist straps tighter in an attempt to even out the weight, or make it more comfortable, or have this suck less, but it doesn't help. It's then that it sinks in, an inkling of the actual, physical reality of what I'm going to try to do.

I'm going to try to walk with this pack on my back. Not just walk, but hike. Climb. I am exhausted and I haven't even left the parking lot. And the start of the trail is almost a mile away. I look down the road at the steady stream of hikers heading to the trailhead, which I've learned is the most popular starting point in Yosemite. There are a few other large packs like mine, but most people carry regular daypacks or none at all. There are families with small children, young and old couples, small groups and larger ones that look like they're on some kind of tours. Many carry what look like metal ski poles, and standing here with this pack on my back, I can see why. Any extra help would be worth it. I check that my car is locked one last time, feel for the water tube that hangs over my shoulder, and my phone in the side mesh pocket of the pack, and then I take a deep breath. Here goes nothing. With a few wobbly steps, I join the stream of happy summer hikers.

Almost immediately, I hear a little voice just behind me say, "Whoa, look at *her* backpack, Mama. She must be going a loooonnng way!"

"I bet she is," a woman's voice answers.

I glance backward, but I can't see around my pack. I can still hear the little voice, though.

"Look at all those patches and pins all over it! They're so pretty!"

"I know, they're very cool!" her mom says. Then she

lowers her voice to just above a whisper. "Maybe she's collected them from all of the places she's been," she says. "She looks like an adventurer, just like us."

Seconds later, the little girl, dressed in miniature hiking gear, shuffles up next to me, her tiny legs working hard to keep up with my pace, slow as it is. She looks up at me over the rim of her heart-shaped sunglasses. "I'm going to the top of a waterfall today," she declares proudly.

"Wow," I manage. I slow my pace just a touch. "That's awesome."

Her mom catches up to her and grabs her hand, giving me an apologetic look. "Sorry, she's really excited—and quite impressed with your backpack."

I smile down at the little girl. "You wanna carry it for me?"

This makes her laugh. "No WAY. I have my own backpack." She turns so I can see it. "Are you going to the waterfall too?" she asks me.

I shake my head. "Not exactly."

"Then where are you going? Somewhere far? Is that why your backpack is so ginormous? And are ALL of those patches from places you've been? My mom says they are."

"Lia," her mom says, "too many questions, sweetie." She turns to me. "Sorry. Again. She was admiring all of the patches on your backpack, and we wondered if maybe you'd collected them on other adventures." She glances at her daughter. "We're very big on adventures right now."

"That's great," I say, not sure what else to add. I didn't think about it until she said it, but I bet she's right about the patches, and all of the places *Bri* had been.

For a long moment, nobody seems to know what to say next, and the silence is made even more awkward by the fact that we've fallen into the same pace. The sound of our boots and breathing seem to grow louder until Lia breaks the silence with more questions.

"So are you going somewhere new? And far?"

Her curious, little-girlness makes me smile.

"Yes," I say. "Both. Somewhere new—and far."

"Where? How far?"

"To the top of Mount Whitney." I don't know why I say it. As soon as the words come out of my mouth, I feel like the worst kind of liar.

"Wow," her mom says. "That *is* far. That's the whole John Muir Trail, right?"

I nod.

"How far is it?" Lia asks excitedly.

I picture the first page of Bri's journal. Her handwriting. "Two hundred and eleven miles."

Lia's jaw drops. "By *yourself*? Don't you have anyone to go with? Won't you get lonely? What about at night? Aren't you gonna be scared?"

"*Lia*," her mom says, "that's not polite."

But even as she says it, she looks at me with a new level of concern in her eyes, like she wants to know the answers too. It makes me think of my mom, and how worried she'll be when she gets home and finds my note.

"Yes, I'm going by myself," I say. "But I won't be lonely." I look at Lia. "It's good to be with just yourself sometimes."

She's quiet a moment as we walk, like she's turning the idea around in her mind. And now it's her mom who speaks.

"It was Muir, wasn't it? Who said that going out is really going in? Something to that effect?"

I have no idea what she means, but seeing as I'm going to hike the trail named after the man, I nod.

"I think it was," she says. She looks at me now. "It's good to take time like that—to get out, clear your head, listen to your thoughts. I never would've been brave enough to do that on my own at your age. It's impressive." She says to Lia, "Isn't what she's doing so cool?"

"Yeah!" Lia agrees. "You must be SO brave. And superstrong."

All of a sudden I want out of this conversation because I am not brave or strong. And I'm already lonely. And now I'm a shaky, sweaty mess who's trying to figure out how to justify quitting before I even begin while lying to this little girl and her mom.

"I bet you'll be even braver one day," I manage to say

to Lia before I pick up my pace the slightest bit. "You two enjoy the waterfall, okay?"

"Good luck to you," her mom calls. "I hope you find what you're looking for out there." She takes her daughter's hand again, slowing their pace just enough to let me go on my way with only my self-loathing as company.

I look down and focus on putting one foot in front of the other to put some distance between us, but that just makes it worse. This morning, when I'd laced up Bri's boots, I'd been thinking of what my aunt said in her letter about hoping that someday these boots might travel the miles that Bri intended to herself. And standing there in the crisp morning air, I'd felt a tiny flicker of belief that maybe I could make that happen myself.

But watching my feet fight to move her boots and backpack forward makes me feel like an imposter in every possible way. I haven't even made it a mile in her shoes—let alone two hundred and eleven—and I want to turn around before I get any farther. Quit before I fail any bigger. If I stopped right now, I could get back to my car and make it home by the afternoon, like I told my mom I would. Go back to my life without anyone ever knowing what I was almost stupid enough to try.

I veer to the edge of the trail so that I can wait for a break in the hikers to make the turnaround, but when I see Lia and her mom catching up quickly, I don't think I can do it.

Not in front of them. Not after what I told them. Especially not before we even make it to the real trail. I try to think of excuses I could make as I pass them, going the opposite way. That I forgot to lock my car. Or I left something vital behind. But they sound just as hollow as they are, and I can't stomach the thought of lying to that little girl and her mom again after they'd so easily believed what I'd told them just a few minutes ago.

Lia waves when she spots me, and now I really can't quit. So I wave back, then turn around and keep going. I try to find a rhythm, but the way the weight of the pack shifts as I move makes every step feel clumsy. I'd gotten everything back into it after spreading the contents out on the living room floor, but it had taken wedging, and shoving, and cramming it all into every available space. Sharp points and hard edges dig into me at odd angles with each step, but at this point, there's nothing I can do to fix it. So I walk. And walk. And after what feels like miles, I make it to the Happy Isles Bridge, on the other side of which lies the trailhead.

It's not lost on me as I cross the bridge and the roaring river beneath it that I have walked exactly one mile of flat, paved trail and already my legs feel weak. When I reach the other side of the bridge, I have to step aside so an elderly man with a walking stick can pass me. It takes a few moments to catch my breath, so I pretend to study the wooden sign that is the official beginning of the trail. At first, I'm confused by the title: High Sierra Loop Trail. But beneath it are two columns that list the names of places and their distances, both in miles and kilometers. My eyes travel all the way down to the end, where I find Bri's destination:

Mount Whitney via John Muir Trail 211 miles

I can't begin to think about that at this point so I bring my eyes up to the listing for the first stop on her itinerary instead:

CLOUDS REST 10 miles

Ten and a half miles. It's farther than I've ever walked, but I just made it one mile without dying, so maybe it's not *completely* impossible. Maybe I can make it there, to that first place she wanted to go—the one from the picture—just to see it for myself. I can stand on top of that mountain like she did, and maybe somehow, that'll be enough. Maybe I'll feel good about it.

I want to feel good about something today.

It seems like there should be some sense of ceremony, or a way to mark the beginning of this thing I've just made up my mind to do. I wrangle my phone out of the side pocket of the pack and look around for someone to take my picture in front of the sign before I take the real first step of this hike. But there's no one nearby. I stand to the side of the sign and hold my camera out as far as I can to take a selfie, but I can't get it all in the frame.

Finally, I step back and settle on taking a picture of just the sign. In my mind, I think of all the different captions I could post with it to tell people what I'm doing so I wouldn't be the only one who knows. Because right now, besides the few strangers I've talked to about it, there is no one else who does, and that is a lonely, lonely feeling.

For a second, I think about how quickly I could set up a new account under a different name, and start posting pictures of this trip. I think of Bri's feed—the scrapbook she left behind—and I picture how my new one could be more like hers. It could be full of inspirational posts about going outside and seeking adventure. I see the whole trip spread out in front of me—a series of anticipated memories and posts of beautiful scenery, and meaningful captions, all of it adding up to show how much I've grown and changed. But then I realize that under a new name, no one would even know to follow me. And that's not the point of this whole thing anyway.

Getting away from all that was the point.

I stow my phone and look at the sign one more time. Ten and a half miles. I can make it there to that place where my cousin stood in the picture, where she looked so free and happy. And maybe by the time I get there, I'll feel that way too.

"Okay," I say under my breath, "here we go," and then I step onto the trail she has led me to.

It surprises me that it's asphalt, and for the first little bit I even think it might not be so bad after all. Trees and ferns in every shade of green line the walkway that skirts the river's edge, and the sunlight filters its way down through the high branches to where it dances on the ground in front of me. It's pretty, and calm, and I try to appreciate the beauty around me to distract myself from the weight of the pack.

And then the trail begins to climb, and I stop noticing the scenery. Up and up it goes, high above the river, but still so far below the granite peaks above. Again, I try to find a rhythm to walking like this, but leaned forward as I am, under the weight of the pack, it's impossible. Every step is a strain, and I can't help but wonder what the hell Bri was thinking. What anyone is thinking when they decide to do this. It's hard, and already monotonous, and I don't want to, but I keep going because a little ways up the trail, I can see a bridge that crosses a river, and people, and even a bathroom. This gives me a little hope. There are lots of people who do this, and I haven't really left civilization yet.

When I get to the bridge, the view is so beautiful I decide to rest there a minute. I lean against the railing and look up at the waterfall that tumbles over dark granite rock farther up the mountain. It sends mist up into the air in every direction, like it's raining upward. When I turn, my eyes follow the river down the canyon until it disappears into the trees and continues to where I began. The distance looks vast, but the sign informs me that I am at the Vernal Falls Bridge, exactly .8 miles from the beginning trail, bringing my grand total to 1.9 miles.

I try not to be disappointed. I keep going, past where the trail splits and the asphalt ends, and where I find out the real work begins. The trail turns to sandy, rocky switchbacks that seem to go on forever under the midday sun. I stop for water and to rest at the corner of each one. Hikers in daypacks pass me at lightning speed. Some say hello. Others nod their greeting. I do the same. One girl who is coming down the trail from the opposite direction meets my eyes then looks at my pack. When we pass each other, she puts a hand out, like you would for a high five. I raise mine to meet it.

"You got this, girl," she says. "The view from the top's worth it. Keep going." And then she releases my hand and does just that. And so do I, buoyed the tiniest bit by a stranger's encouragement.

A short distance from there, the trail drops into Little Yosemite Valley, according to the sign, and skirts along a meadow and riverbank in the first flat section I've passed through. The lack of incline feels like a reprieve to my shaky legs, and when I reach the bank of the deep, lazy river, I decide to stop and take off the pack for a few moments.

They are blissful moments, despite the fact that I am utterly exhausted. And thirsty. I walk my almost-empty water bottle to the spout to fill up, surprised at how much I've already gone through after only a few miles. After, I find a shaded log to sit on and dig into the pack for something to eat, because all of a sudden I'm starving too. I grab the first thing I can find, then sit there with the bag of trail mix, alone in the middle of the towering pine trees, with the sun filtering down through them in visible beams, and it is so, so quiet. I close my eyes.

I remember this kind of quiet.

It's the same kind Bri and I would find deep in the woods behind her house, when we'd go adventuring as kids. We'd pretend we were lost and instead of trying to find our way home, we'd have to survive out in the forest, relying only on what we could find and the things we knew how to do. We'd build makeshift shelters of branches and pine needles, then pile rocks in a ring and make a pretend fire to crouch beside. She'd climb high in the trees, pretending to pick fruit, but really just loving the feeling of seeing how far up she could go. I always stayed on the ground, wanting to join her but too scared to try. Never once did she make me feel bad for where I stood. She'd just point out the beauty there too. A butterfly landing on a branch, a leaf she'd set loose, twirling to the ground. The sun shining down through the trees.

I open my eyes, and it's there, that same light. And for a second, it feels like she's there too.

"I'm here!" I say out loud. "Doing this crazy-ass thing you were supposed to do."

The hush of a breeze moves through the treetops like an answer.

"*We* were supposed to do," I whisper.

A tiny blue butterfly lands silently on the log where I sit. When I reach for it, it takes flight, weaving a spiraling path up a beam of sunlight.

I watch until it disappears into the trees. Then I stand, blow a kiss upward, and put the pack back on to keep going, into a forest so deep I can't see the sky.

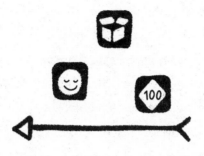

CLOUDS REST

LATE AFTERNOON.

I emerge from the trees, sweating and exhausted, and stop to catch my breath. In front of me is a granite ridge that juts straight up in the sky, towering over the valley below. My eyes follow the ridge upward to where it narrows into what looks like a rocky staircase leading nowhere. A stiff wind rises against me and I wonder how in the world I'm allowed to be here, doing this. I shouldn't be. I don't know what I'm doing, only that this looks like the place from Bri's journal, and that the two people who passed me on their way back down from the summit confirmed that yes, I am standing at the base of Clouds Rest, yes, it's worth the view to hike the last half mile, and yes, it's safe. Relatively. Just as long as I stay on the ridge and don't go plunging down to the valley from the peak, which is a towering 9,926 feet.

No wonder I can't breathe.

I look up to where the rocky stairs seem to disappear into the top of the ridge, take a shaky breath, and then focus on the path in front of me, and Bri's boots, and putting one in front of the other. My legs ache like they never have before, but at the suggestion of the two friendly hikers who passed me, I left my pack a few yards back, so I feel a little lighter and more balanced at least. It's a relief and a form of motivation. I only have to carry myself up this ridge. Which I work on doing, very carefully.

I walk, and the only sounds up here are of the wind, and the crunch of my boots on the gravelly trail. And my breathing, which is more labored than it has been all day. The air feels thin, and I can't seem to get enough to fill my lungs. Still, I keep going. I can feel I'm almost there.

The ridge begins to narrow, and I reach a point where I can see I'm going to have to climb and pull myself up between two boulders because there is no way around them. I look around at the drop-off on either side then swallow and wedge my feet between the rocks. My heart pounds in my chest, and I try to focus on finding a hold for my hands so I can pull myself up. I scan the rocks on either side of me and find the smallest of indentations for my fingers. Slowly, I put all of my weight onto the foot that's wedged between the boulders, and then I summon all my strength and resolve to pull myself up by my fingers, which now grip the rocks so hard my arms shake uncontrollably.

I go for it, and my foot slips.

And then I'm falling, knocking and scraping my limbs on the granite that held me up moments ago. I hit the ground behind me with a thud and a whimper, shocked at the hardness of my landing. Silence follows, and I look down at my knees, brush off the gravel. Tiny pinpricks of red bloom as blood rises to the surface of the thin skin. My nails are jagged and torn from trying to hold on as I went scraping down the rock.

I'm shaken, but intact. Mostly. I look around instinctively for someone—anyone else. But I am alone. High above me in the sky, a bird circles in slow motion, and the wind blows, and the sun shines down, unblinking, like nothing happened. I realize in this moment how inconsequential I am out here. The mountains and the sky have no sympathy for my pain or stupidity. It's just me, and what to do next is up to me.

I look back up at the two boulders—at the seemingly insurmountable obstacles in front of me, and I feel angry. Angry at Bri for putting me out here, at myself for being weak, at the world for being as it is. I'm angry at all of it because now I have a choice: turn around and quit, or try again. I don't want to do either one. I want to be somewhere else, relaxing in my room, scrolling through my phone, looking at things like this from a safe, comfortable distance. But instead, I'm here on this mountain, wearing my cousin's boots that are already giving me blisters.

I get to my feet and dig, with the last bit of resolve I have, for the last bit of strength in me. And I decide to try again. This time, I find a better foothold and am able to haul myself up over the rocks with shaky arms. I drag my legs up and over, and there I am, on the other side of the boulders. I look back, surprised. I hadn't expected to make it on this try either. If I had the energy to laugh, I would. I think of the first page of Bri's journal. Maybe *I'm* stronger than I let myself believe.

I sit there on top of the boulder, surveying the narrow bridge of rock stretched out in front of me. It's not until then that it hits me. I've made it. I am at the summit of Clouds Rest, the first destination of Bri's journey.

And now I don't know what to do next.

I climb down from the rocks and walk—slowly, slowly, out onto the bridge in the sky. It's quiet, except for the rush of wind as it pours over the rocks then drops back out into the emptiness below. Still shaken, I look down at my bloodied knees, then at the smooth granite of the ridge beneath my feet. Around me, the sky stretches out vivid blue and boundless in every direction. In the distance, wispy clouds hang over the surrounding mountains and fading jet trails crisscross the sky.

I stand a moment longer, trying to catch my breath as the sting of my cuts begins to subside. And then, without warning, I start to cry. Not because it's so beautiful here, and not because I'm so happy to have made it, but because I don't have the strength left in my arms to lift them up like Bri did in her picture. I am hurt and exhausted, and I don't feel the joy or the freedom that I always saw in her.

Standing here, in the place my cousin was supposed to be standing today, with my knees bleeding and my hands shaking, I feel more acutely alone than I ever have in my life.

It's not what I was expecting.

I look down at her boots on my feet, like they might offer some insight or guidance, and that's when I notice the small, round medallion on the ground in front of me. The skin on my knees stings as I squat down to get a closer look. Engraved in the bronze is an arrow, along with the stamp of the US Geological Survey. It's dated 1956. I run my fingers over it, and wonder for a brief moment about the person who put it there, and why they would bother to hike up this ridge and mark it. The medallion isn't big or showy. It doesn't give any other information. Really, you could walk right over it and not even notice it was there. But it's been here for over sixty years, quietly marking this place. An acknowledgment that people come here. I think of all the people who have, my cousin included, and for a second I feel a little bit of connection to something.

I stand again and take my phone out of my pocket, then place my feet on either side of the medallion, and take a picture, marking that we made it here. I wish I had something better, or more meaningful to do, but this is the best I've got. I look around at the surreal landscape. What do people do at the top of a mountain like this? Celebrate? Meditate? Go back down? That seems so anticlimactic.

And then I remember something. At the end of every adventure we took, Bri had a tradition. We each had to find something tiny—a pebble, or a leaf, or maybe a mini pinecone, to bring back with us so we'd remember the day. Usually tired, and wanting to go home, I always made my choice quickly and based on proximity. I'd grab whatever small thing was nearby then shove it in my pocket, only to be forgotten and lost in the laundry later. Bri took her time choosing, though, and she cherished each little bit of nature she brought home with her. Her windowsills and shelves were always lined with these objects, and she could tell you the story of each one—what the day was like, where she found it, why she chose it.

I look down at the ground for something she might choose. There are no plants up here on this ridge, and the gravel all around is really just little pieces of granite, chipped off the gray rock where I stand. This seems fitting. To take a piece of Clouds Rest. I crouch to choose one, and when the sun glints off a piece with a shiny fleck of something metallic, I decide it's the one and put it in my pocket to carry with me.

I'm so stiff and sore that it takes me a moment to stand back up, and when I do, I try to soak in the view, and to feel some shift in perspective or enlightening moment, but it feels forced. So I do what I normally would do. I lift my phone and take a panoramic picture of the sky and the mountains, careful to get the iconic silhouette of Half Dome as a point of reference in case I ever do post the picture anywhere. And then I flip the lens and take a shot of myself standing at the top of this mountain because that's what you do when you go somewhere. You take a selfie and then you post it for everyone to see and comment on, and that's how you know that what you did matters. I laugh. Out here that world feels far away, like a made-up story, but I try to imagine what I would say anyway, if I were to post a picture from today. Nothing comes, though. I'm too tired for even that.

The sun hangs low in the sky, and I know from Bri's journal that she'd planned to watch the sunset from this point right here, but I can feel the air growing colder, chilling my damp clothes as it does. Every muscle in me is sapped, and I ache all the way down in my bones, so I give the view one last look, then turn and work my way back down to where I left Bri's pack.

I'm confused at first when I see some of its contents strewn around on the rocks. What kind of person would go through another hiker's pack like that? But as I get closer, I realize it wasn't a person. It was a cat-sized, furry animal whose name I don't know, and who happens to be still here, happily munching on one of the protein bars from the top pocket.

"Hey!" I lunge toward it, and it startles and runs—carrying the plundered bar with it.

For all I know, that bar was supposed to count for a whole meal, but I'm too tired to care. I pick up the empty baggie and the water bottle that now has teeth marks on it, then set to work finding a spot to pitch my tent, which I don't know how to do. The sun hasn't even touched the tops of the mountains yet, but I don't know how long it's going to take me to figure out the whole tent thing, and I definitely don't want to be without one when it gets dark.

After a few attempts, I surprise myself and I figure it out, and soon I am the proud occupant of a tiny, orange, nylon cave. I lay out the bedroll and drag the pack inside, where it takes up most of the space, then I sit there in the fading light, unsure of what comes next. I'm too tired to eat, but I know I should, so I finish off a protein bar, stow the wrapper in the bear canister, then double-check that all food and anything that could possibly have a scent is inside of it.

I swallow some Advil, take a few more sips of water. Sit in the quiet of my home for the night.

I'm tempted to just crawl into the sleeping bag as I am, but I can tell I need to deal with my feet first. I take a deep breath and ease them slowly out of Bri's boots, one at a time, wincing at the pain of what lies beneath my socks. I'm afraid to peel them away and see the damage that I can feel, but if I want to make it back tomorrow, I don't have a choice. Off come the socks too.

I've had plenty of blisters before, but nothing prepares me for the sight of my feet after the day's hike. The skin of both Achilles looks like it's been dragged across a cheese grater, and now I realize that's what it feels like too. I reach for the tube of antibiotic ointment and dab it gingerly over the angry, red skin, then cover each heel with a bandage, because that's all I have the energy to do. And then I lie back on the sleeping bag to catch my breath.

Above me, I can see the sky through the thin mesh that I didn't bother to put the cover over because it felt too claustrophobic. I look up at my little patch of twilight sky, and try to think about the day, and what it means that I made it this far. It makes me wonder about tomorrow, and what Bri was going to do on Day 2.

I sit up and dig her journal out of the pack and flip to the page to find out. At first it doesn't make sense, and I'm sure I'm reading things wrong. Misunderstanding something. I grab the guidebook and check and recheck it against Bri's next entry that begins with: rejoin the JMT. I puzzle over the map in the orangey light of the tent, tracing my finger along the red dotted line that is the John Muir Trail, reading the names of destinations as I go. It's not until my eyes wander away from the line that I realize a key point my cousin didn't feel she needed to mention in her journal: the hike to Clouds Rest was a detour.

She was going to begin the journey of two hundred and eleven miles with a ten-mile detour.

I want to cry, but then I think about the post she wrote about hitchhiking to Canada, and her response to everyone who told her she was crazy: "You were right, but hey, I still made it."

And I laugh instead. Then I take the pen from its leather loop and write at the bottom of Day 1.

I made it too.

I'LL TRY

IT'S DARK WHEN the wind wakes me. It seems to come from all directions, blowing against the sides of my tent and lifting the flaps as it whips in through the vents beneath. Far above me, it rushes wildly through the trees. They creak and groan in a way that makes me wish I hadn't pitched my tent beneath them. I sit up straight, heart pounding, and listen to the chaos outside, and it hits me how completely helpless I am in this moment.

There isn't anyone I can ask for help. No one to tell me it'll be okay. And I have no idea what to do. A sudden gust hits the tent with a force that sends my heart up into my throat, and I cover my mouth to keep from crying out. I grab the small flashlight and the pocketknife that I laid next to my head, and then I fumble around for my phone like somehow these things will keep me safe as I burrow down into the sleeping bag to wait it out.

All I can think is that I hope it's almost morning, so I can get up and pack and get out of here and back to my room, with its bed surrounded by four solid walls, protected from all of the elements outside of them. Right now I don't care what Bri wrote about not wanting to wake up in the same house every morning. I'd give anything to be there and never have to experience this again.

I try to stay calm, and I try not cry, but I fail at both when the next gust hits. There is nothing else to do. With the sleeping bag pulled tight around me, I curl into a ball beneath it and listen to the howl of the wind drown out the sound of my own tears.

I don't know how much time goes by, but I drift in and out of sleep until eventually the wind settles, and darkness becomes softer around the edges. And then, out of nowhere and everywhere, complete silence descends. It's a silence like none I've heard before, and it makes me sit up and take notice, because all of a sudden I realize something: I made it through the night.

I also realize how badly I have to pee after holding it through the night and the windstorm, so from where I sit, I fish out yesterday's stiff socks from the boots where

I tucked them. They scrape against my skin as I pull them over my feet, and I dig in the pack for a pair of sandals I've seen somewhere in the jumble. It's not a look I would ever attempt in civilization, but I can't think about forcing my sore feet into the hiking boots yet, and there's no one around to see anyway. I unzip the little half-moon door and crawl out, a movement that immediately informs me that there is not a fiber of my being that doesn't ache from yesterday's hike. When I hobble away from the tent like an eighty-year-old and squat with shaking legs to do my business, it is a feat in itself.

Back at the tent, I rifle through the bear canister for something suitable for breakfast, though I'm not really hungry, and settle on a baggie of dried fruit. I don't want to be in the tent another moment after last night, so I close everything back up tight in the canister and zip the door shut behind me, then take my breakfast for a walk up the ridge, hoping my muscles will loosen up as I go. The air is cool—cold even, and I shiver a little as I walk. It's hard to believe it's summer, and it makes me realize what a completely different world I'm in than I'm used to inhabiting.

At home, I'd still be sleeping, and by the time I woke up, the day would be well on its way to the typical August heat in Southern California. Here, the sun is just lighting the sky, and judging by what I read in the guidebook last night, there will still be snow on some of the high mountain passes that Bri was planning on crossing.

I shiver again, not wanting to think about what that would be like to hike through, and a second later, when I reach the outlook, I don't think about it. Not at all. Because spread out in front of me is the brilliant sunrise sky, ignited by the sun that still hides behind the jagged peaks. I wish I could take a picture, because it's even more breathtaking than the one I saw the morning I arrived—yesterday, I remind myself, though it seems so distant now too.

I breathe in deep and think about what the ranger said to me, how every day is a fresh start and a chance to be better than you were the day before. As I watch the morning light creep across the mountains, I believe it. Yesterday was brutal and last night was crazy, but I'm here today. And for the first time since I started, the landscape looks almost welcoming, like maybe I could be a part of it the same way Bri was. I have the thought then that maybe I'm not ready to go back just yet. And thanks to Bri and her detour, I have plenty of miles to hike back to the John Muir Trail before I have to make up my mind about that.

Back at my camp, which is really just my tent, I swallow a few more Advil and sit down with Bri's journal to see what's on her itinerary for today, just in case. On the Day 2 page I expect to see mileage and elevation and notes, like there was for Day 1, but that's not what I find. Day 2 begins not with a destination, but a quote:

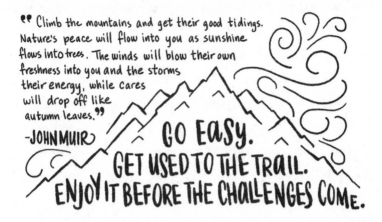

> " Climb the mountains and get their good tidings. Nature's peace will flow into you as sunshine flows into trees. The winds will blow their own freshness into you and the storms their energy, while cares will drop off like autumn leaves. "

—JOHN MUIR

GO EASY.
GET USED TO THE TRAIL.
ENJOY IT BEFORE THE CHALLENGES COME.

There is no mileage goal or place to camp listed. Just this. I read it over again.

Maybe it's the exhaustion after yesterday, or the altitude that has me a little loopy, but the irony of both Bri's and Muir's words strikes me as funny. I definitely don't feel fresh from the wind, and my cares have not so much dropped away as shifted to the most basic things, like making it down this mountain and finding water. Which doesn't bode well for me if the challenges haven't even begun. But then she's not asking a lot for Day 2, and it makes me feel like I don't want to let her down. I slip the pen from its loop and write my answer.

I'll try.

It takes me close to an hour to get ready to go, because I'm determined to do a better job packing. I pull everything out of the pack, and try to remember how it had been arranged when it arrived. When that fails, I look at all of it and think about what would make sense if I were actually going to keep hiking. I start by putting the tent and bedroll down at the bottom of the pack, because I wouldn't need those again until tonight. On top of that, I pack the extra clothes, and then I try to layer everything else in order of importance of accessibility on top of them. By the time I'm finished, the pack actually looks a little less unwieldy than it did yesterday. Which makes me feel a little more experienced than I was then. When I heave the pack onto my shoulders and click the straps around my waist and across my chest, I'm even a little proud.

And then there's nothing left to do but step back onto the trail. I start down the mountain under the assumption that this part will be easier than yesterday, because it's downhill. Very quickly, I realize that I am mistaken. The first thing I notice is the pain and soreness—so much, everywhere, despite the Advil I took before I started. The second is that it feels like I have to push back against gravity and the weight of the pack so that they don't combine forces and send me tumbling down the trail. My toes dig into the fronts of Bri's boots, and I imagine new blisters already beginning to form. My knees take the rest of the burden, and I have to concentrate on keeping them stable as I make my way down the thousands of vertical feet I climbed yesterday.

Down I go, and on the easier parts, I try to look around and notice the scenery, and let my mind wander somewhere else that is pain-free, but the majority of the time, the terrain and the challenge of moving through it demand my full attention. I hike with my eyes down, focused only on the narrow trail in front of me. I don't know how long it takes me because time somehow seems irrelevant here, but by the time the sun is high in the sky, and I finally step foot back onto the John Muir Trail, the feeling is damn near euphoric.

Just off the trail, I spot a perfect rock to rest on. I take off my pack and nearly collapse onto the sun-warmed granite, looking up at the sky. Not one cloud interrupts the clear blue stretched out in every direction above me. I close my eyes and shield my face with my arm, then let the sunlight sink into my skin, and try to picture it like the Muir quote said—like nature's peace flowing in. It almost feels like that. Or maybe it's just exhaustion. Either way, I could drift off to sleep right here on this rock, right now, if I let myself. But I have a decision to make. It's a simple one, really: keep going or turn back. I lie there with my eyes still closed, bouncing back and forth between the two choices.

Keep going or turn back? Keep going or turn back? Keep—

"Bri?" a female voice says out of nowhere. "Is that you?"

Her name is a shot of adrenaline. Immediately, I am on my feet, facing a hiker girl who looks about my age.

"Oh," she says, looking a little startled. "I'm sorry, I thought you were someone I knew." She makes a move to continue on wherever she was heading, but I reach out my hand in front of her.

"You called me Bri," I say.

She nods. "Yeah, I know a girl by that name who has a pack that looks almost exactly like that—all those patches and pins," she says, eyeing Bri's pack resting next to the rock. She pauses, looking down at my hand, which still hovers in the air in front of her.

"How do you know her?" I ask.

"Um . . ." She gives me a wary look. "Do I . . . know you somehow?"

"No," I say. "I'm her cousin."

The girl breaks into a smile. "Ohhhh . . . okay! How IS she?" She looks around. "*Where* is she? She's thru-hiking the trail this summer, right?"

My throat goes dry, and all of a sudden my chest feels tight. "Um." Tears spring to my eyes, and the girl reaches out and grabs my hand now.

"What? What is it?" Worry creases her brow. "Is everything okay?"

I shake my head, and tears spill down my cheeks, and now she takes me by my shoulders, her voice more urgent.

"Did something happen? Is Bri okay?"

I shake my head again, force myself to say the words to this stranger who knew her, but doesn't know about what happened. "No," I say. "She . . . there was an accident, and . . ."

Her face goes pale. "What do you mean? What are you saying?"

"She's gone," I whisper, barely able to get the words out. "She died."

The girl falls to her knees in front of me and crumples forward into the dirt. I don't know what else to do so I drop to my own knees beside her, and put a hand on her backpack. And there, in the middle of the trail, I join a stranger whose name I don't know as she cries for my cousin beneath the cloudless blue sky.

HIKE YOUR OWN HIKE

EVENING. We sit on opposite sides of the campfire Corrie built, and she listens intently as I tell the story of how I ended up here, wearing Bri's backpack and boots, attempting to do at least part of her hike. Or rather, I tell her most of the story. I leave out the part about my social media life because out here, in its absence, I'm even more ashamed of it than I was at home.

But I do tell her that Bri and I had grown apart, and that it was my fault. It feels good to be honest about this, at least, and maybe it's because she doesn't know me, or because she *did* know Bri, but somehow I trust her with this admission. When I get to the part about our shared birthday, and the package arriving, and my crazy decision to drive all the way up here to hike Clouds Rest, she interrupts.

"*Wow*," she says, hugging her arms like she's trying to stay warm. "That is just . . . look." She holds one arm out into the light of the fire, and I can see it's covered in goose bumps.

"I know. It's crazy, and I don't actually think I could do the whole hike, but I thought—"

"I think you can do it," Corrie says firmly. "And not only that, I think you *need* to do it."

"Really?"

"Really. Things like this don't happen without a reason, I truly believe that. And I also think that everyone who comes into our lives leaves us with a gift. I only knew Bri very briefly, but that was definitely the case with her." She smiles. "I think getting you out here to do this was somehow her gift to you. Maybe even a chance for you two to find your way back to each other."

I blink back the tears that spring to my eyes because she's just put into words something that feels like it could be true.

"What was her gift to you?" I ask.

The fire crackles between us, and we both watch the flames as she thinks about it for a few moments. Finally, she looks at me in the orangey glow.

"She taught me to hike my own hike."

She takes a deep breath and leans back on her pack. "When I met her, I had just come back from my first

Mount Whitney attempt. I was the only one in my party who hadn't made it to the summit, and I was totally distraught about failing at what so many other people were able to do. Especially because I'd been so obsessed with doing everything right. I'd bought all the highest-rated equipment, read every blog and guide I could find, watched all the videos on YouTube, done the training hikes, but none of that had mattered once I got out there on the trail and tried to keep up with everyone else who was way more experienced than me. I just couldn't do it. The pace and the altitude got to me."

For a moment, I can see the memory of that disappointment flash over her face, but then she smiles.

"I met Bri a few weeks after that, here in Yosemite. We were both waiting around at the permit office for the Half Dome cables permit lottery—those permits are nearly impossible to get through reservation, but they hold back a few for hikers who show up the day of, and draw a few lucky names each day. Neither one of us won a permit, and I was so upset, because somehow, in my mind, doing Half Dome was going to redeem my Mount Whitney fail. But it didn't faze Bri. She just shrugged it off, and invited me to hike to Clouds Rest with her instead."

Now it's me who has the goose bumps.

"And it was the best hike I'd ever been on. She wasn't worried about pace or miles, or anything other than just being out there, and so neither was I. It was so different from what I was used to, but it was exactly what I needed to learn. It's hard to explain, but she wandered more than she hiked." She pauses and smiles like she's remembering. "She had this natural, easy flow to how she moved through nature." Her voice breaks a little, and she pauses again to compose herself. "That's how I thought of her trail name that day."

"Her what?"

"It's a nickname you go by out on the trail. Usually other hikers give it to you as kind of a rite of passage. Sometimes it's a funny joke. Other times, it's just something that describes you."

"What did you call her?" I ask softly.

"Butterfly," she says.

I flash back to the violet-blue butterfly I saw in the forest just yesterday, and then I look at Corrie and smile.

"You got her exactly right."

We sit beside the fire until only the glowing embers are left, talking like old friends. I tell stories of Bri and me as kids, and Corrie tells me about growing up in the mountains, and learning to hike on her own. She shows me how to work the stove, and explains the right way to use the water filter. We take out my guidebook, and in the light of our headlamps, she goes over sections of the trail that will be difficult, explaining how to cross creeks, and what to do when I hit the snow. She teaches me a system for washing and rotating my clothes, and caring for my blisters. By the time we zip ourselves into our tents for the night, I feel overwhelmed at the magnitude of what lies in front of me, but a little more prepared to meet it.

The next morning, we rise early and watch the sun emerge from behind the distant peaks. After, it's time to break camp and head our separate ways. I'm sad that Corrie and I are headed in opposite directions, but so grateful that our trails crossed, and for the gifts she's given me.

I'm kneeling on the ground, zipping the final items into Bri's pack, when I notice a small butterfly pin on one of the pocket flaps. I take it off, then dig the journal out of the pack and open to the place where I've tucked the picture of Bri standing on top of Clouds Rest, and I bring them both over to Corrie, who is finishing up with her own pack.

"I have something for you," I say, holding out the picture.

She gasps, and reaches for it. "Oh my gosh, I took this picture. That day, I took this picture of her with her phone." She points at it, then looks at me like she can't believe it.

"I wondered about that last night," I say. I hold out the butterfly pin between us. "This was on her pack. I think you should have it to put on yours."

I hand it to her, and tears spring to her eyes. "Really? Are you sure?"

"You gave her the name."

She pulls me into a hug. "Thank you. You have no idea how much this means—of course I'll put it on my pack." She looks around. "I wish I had something to give you."

"You've already given me more than you know," I say, and I mean it. Not just the tips and the encouragement, but a snapshot of Bri as she was out here.

Corrie releases me from the hug and holds on to my shoulders. "I know you can do this, Mari. Be brave, and remember that you're not just doing it for her, it's for you too. So hike your own hike."

We say our good-byes, and I watch her go until she disappears around the bend of the trail. And then it's just me. And the moment I choose to take what feels like my *real* first step onto the John Muir Trail. I am really doing this.

I hike. I follow the trail as it winds through thick forests and up and down steep switchbacks. When I reach the first place where the trail ends on one side of a creek and picks up again on the other, and no one has built a bridge to cross it, I do exactly what Corrie instructed: I take my shoes off and switch to the sandals, then plunge my feet into the icy water. And I make it to the other side. I have to do this so many times on this section of trail that I lose count.

In other places, fallen trees block the trail, forcing me to either climb over or crawl under the massive trunks. Over and over I am confronted with obstacles or choices I don't want to make but have to if I want to keep moving forward. Here, there is no tuning reality out or letting it fade into the background, or obsessing over meaningless things. The immediacy of being on the trail is real. It demands my concentration, and it's both mentally exhausting and physically taxing.

I don't see another person for miles, and by midday, my only thoughts are an endless loop comprised of two conflicting desires: to move forward and to stop and rest. The two ideas play tug-of-war in my head, and I hold out and just keep moving for as long as I can, wanting to make it to the third day goal listed in Bri's journal. But then I remember what Corrie said about her Whitney attempt, and pushing too hard, and what Bri wrote, about enjoying the journey, and I think I'd enjoy it a lot more after some food, water, and a short rest.

I find a place just off the trail that overlooks yet another mountain vista, and I stop there, eagerly anticipating the feeling of dropping my pack. The relief is immediate when I do, and I smile and stretch in the sunlight. After a few sips of warm water, I dig into the pack for the bear canister and my hands can hardly open it fast enough. The first thing I see is a bag full of smaller baggies with portioned-out nuts inside. I grab two of them, then spot another promising-looking bag packed the same way—this one containing what looks like jerky, vegan diet be damned. I scan the contents of the canister for anything else, and when I spot a bag full of fun-size Snickers bars, I think I've maybe died and gone to heaven. But these things need to last, so I just take one and save it for my dessert.

I find myself a nice flat rock to sit on and spread what feels like a feast out in front of me, along with my water bottle, and I sit there in the midday sun, at the top of a ridge whose name I don't know, inhaling food I never would in my normal life, and it's amazing. I honestly can't think of another time food tasted so good. I sit there chewing the salty jerky and cashews, thinking about how, for so long, I've worried about food, rather than enjoyed it. For all my pictures, it was either about how pretty a meal looked for a photo, or how many calories were in it and how that would make *me* look in the next photo. Sitting here on this rock, savoring the taste of every bite I take, I marvel at how little time it has taken those old worries to feel distant and foolish. I am sore and tired and stinky right now, but I am infinitely more comfortable with myself in this moment than I have been for a long time. I'm not sucked in or pushed up or worrying about any tiny bulge that might be showing through my yoga pants.

I just am. And that is enough.

I can't think of the last time I felt like this, where I wasn't striving or stressing about my body. These last few years, the focus of my accounts became all about how I looked. How thin I was, how tan I was, how fit I was. I hid behind the excuse of wanting to live a healthy life, but that's not what I was doing at all. I was obsessing about calories and exercising excessively, and so hungry—for nourishment, and for affirmation. Every time I got the slightest bit—a comment about how beautiful I was, or thin I was—I wanted more. And after a little while, it wasn't enough.

Today, despite the pain in my bones and muscles, I feel better. And freer. It makes me think of Bri and how beautiful I always thought she was. She was confident and strong, comfortable in her own skin even though she wasn't stick thin like I worked so hard to be. She didn't wear a lot of makeup or trendy clothes. In most of her pictures, her sun-drenched hair hangs long and natural, and the apples of her cheeks sport the bright pink evidence of days spent beneath the sun.

But it's her joy that really shines in those photos. Her smile. The warmth and life there. When I compare it in my mind to all of the carefully posed and edited shots on my own feed, the difference between us makes me sad. I feel a pang of shame again—at myself, and the things I put so much effort into. Things I thought mattered. I've wasted so much time, and so much of *me* on them.

I think of Bri's words in her journal: *I only have so much time, and I won't waste a second. I want to see it all, I want to make a difference in people's lives, and I want to be happy.*

I believe she was happy. She was going out and doing exactly what she said, living life the way she wanted to. I think of all the people who wrote about her and the difference she made in their lives. How she helped them and made an impact without even realizing it. And somehow she got me out here, maybe to help me do the same thing. I hope so. Maybe even I can somehow do it all and make a difference in other people's lives too. Those seem like tangible goals. But being happy, that's so much more complicated.

That night at camp, I experience a moment of true happiness when I get the little stove to light on my own. To celebrate, I cook my first hot dinner on the trail—a steaming mug of ramen noodles. I eat every last one and drink all of the salty broth too. After dinner, I wash my mug in a nearby creek, crawl into the sleeping bag, and switch on the headlamp to read the guidebook and see what tomorrow has in store, but immediately I realize I'm too tired even for that. So instead, I lie back on the small backpacking pillow, close my eyes, let myself drift off to the soft sound of water flowing over rocks.

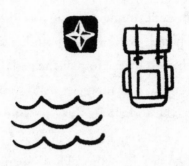

BRI WOULD GO

This is the only thing on the itinerary for Day 4 in Bri's journal. Beneath it is a quote:

> " Fear not, therefore, to try the mountain-passes.
> They will kill care, save you from deadly apathy.
> Set you free…" — JOHN MUIR

I try to hold on to this sentiment, but this is the day my new reality finally sets in—I decide I hate hiking. My body is beaten down, and I'm not sure how far Thousand Island Lake is, or if I'll even make it there. I've already had to cross too many icy rivers to count, one of which swept away the extra pair of socks I had hanging on my pack to dry, and I am about to climb Donohue Pass, the first big one of the hike.

To say I'm dreading it is an understatement.

The snow patches along the trail have become larger and more frequent as I climb higher, which only adds to the general sense of foreboding I feel approaching this first pass. And the switchbacks. I hate them. The effort of crisscrossing the face of a mountain, especially when the "trail" is all broken granite slabs with sandy passageways through them feels like a special kind of torture.

But soon enough I find out there's something even worse. I reach the pass, where the mountain stands up even steeper. Far below is a jagged ravine. At the bottom of which, a rushing ice-blue river churns a stark reminder to tread carefully.

I know what one wrong step can do.

I stop to take a deep breath, because my heart is racing, but also because at this point the trail disappears into snow. In every direction, everywhere I look is a blanket of white, broken up only by steely colored rocks that jut out of the snow in defiance. Beneath the midday sun, it's blinding, even with sunglasses on. I raise my hand to shade my eyes as they sweep over the sea of white in front of me.

This can't be right. People don't do this. I can't *hike* this.

And then, from a distance, I hear something I haven't heard in a whole day. It startles me at first, but then I realize what it is. A voice. Someone is yelling.

I scan the snow to see where it's coming from, and there's a loud whoop, followed by several shouts. When I follow the sound with my eyes, I find them—the tiny dots way up the mountain. *People.*

I don't know whether to cry tears of joy or call out to them for help. They're too far away, probably wouldn't hear me, but I try anyway, desperate for contact, or confirmation, or both.

"HELLO!!!!" I yell. My voice sounds foreign to me, and it bounces back off the snow and the mountains.

The only answer is my own.

I wave my arms and try again. "HELLO!!!"

Some sound must reach them because one of the spots waves back, and then they all do.

"HELLO!" a faraway voice yells back.

I cup my hands to my mouth again, ecstatic. "HOW . . . DID YOU . . . GET THERE?"

There's no answer at first, and I imagine my words being unintelligible sounds by the time they echo off the mountain walls and reach them.

But then a voice comes back, loud and male, the words spaced out like he needs to take a breath between each one: "FOLLOW . . . THE . . . TRACKS . . ."

I glance down and search the bright whiteness for anything that resembles a track or footprint. It takes me a few back-and-forths over the snow, but once my eyes adjust to looking directly at it, I think I see something. I follow the faint, barely discernable lines that cut an indistinct trail through the snow until I lose them. It's not much, but it's more than I had just a moment ago.

"THANK . . . YOU!" I yell back up.

The response comes a few seconds later. "WELCOME!" is all it says, and I'm a little disappointed. I don't know what I was hoping for—an invitation to join them? For them to say they'd wait for me?

I feel that pitiful, lonely feeling again. That, and envy. Envy that whoever they are, they're not alone, and that they're far above me on the mountain. I sigh. Once again, I'm faced with the choice that has been my constant companion on this hike: turn back or keep going. I'm too far in for it really to be a choice, but I take a minute like I'm deciding anyway. I breathe, sip some water, and try to mentally prepare myself to tackle what looks like it is going to be the hardest thing I've come up against yet. Then I attach the crampons to my boots, like Corrie showed me.

Looking at the vast snowfield in front of me, I understand what Bri meant about enjoying the trail before the real challenges start. And right away, I realize she was right. The very first step I take onto the snow pitches me forward when my boot sinks and throws me off balance so that I have to catch myself with both hands. The snow is rough and prickles against my palms, and I crouch there, trying to push myself up. It's only by some miracle that my pack doesn't go over my head and topple me altogether, sinking me deep into the snow that feels like quicksand around my boots, even with the crampons attached.

It bogs my feet down, makes them impossibly heavy. Not to mention the cold that starts to sink into my boots. It's a strange sensation when the rest of me is sweating with effort beneath the high August sun. The heat beats down from above, and the snow pulls and pulls at me from below, and every step is a whole new circle of hell.

I make my way at a snail's pace, losing and finding the tracks, alternating between disbelief and flat-out hatred for what I'm doing. Every so often I stop to rest and look back at the sobering view of the steep mountainside and icy blue river below me. At first, my progress is barely visible, but after a while I can see that I really am climbing this snowy mountain. I am moving myself, albeit achingly slowly, up its steep face with my own two feet. The realization doesn't make me hate it any less, but there is a small measure of satisfaction in it. Never in my previous life would I have imagined doing this, or even thought it possible. And yet here I am, inching my way to the top.

I look down at the tracks in front of me and concentrate on my breathing, which is labored and thin this high up. I know from the guide that the top point of the pass is just over eleven thousand feet, and I must be close, because I can feel the altitude in every breath I take. Together with the crunch of my boots, my breathing makes up a pathetic, uneven non-rhythm. I'm so focused on it, so in my own little world, that when a voice speaks to me, it takes a second to register.

"You have something against using trekking poles?" the voice asks.

I raise my eyes slowly, too spent to be startled. Standing a few steps in front of me is a guy who looks vaguely familiar. He holds out a set of poles like the ones I've seen so many other hikers carrying.

"Wanna try 'em?" he asks. "We're almost there, but this last bit's no joke."

He smiles, and I know right away where I know him from. The Wilderness Office. The one who cleared the way through the group of hikers, for me to get outside.

I stop. "Um . . ." I'm still not used to the way everyone skips any small talk and speaks to each other with such a degree of familiarity out here.

"Sorry." He takes a step toward me and reaches out his free hand. "I'm Josh. I think we sorta met back at the Wilderness Office."

"Mari," I say, taking it. "We sort of did."

He looks around. "Where's your . . . Weren't you gonna be hiking with another girl?"

"No, I—" and then I remember telling the guy there that Bri was outside with our stuff and the conversation that followed. Interesting that he was listening. "She had to bow out," I say, not wanting to elaborate while we're on the side of this mountain.

He raises his eyebrows. "Wow, so it's just you? Solo?"

"Yeah."

"That's pretty badass."

"Not exactly," I say. I glance around, wanting to take the focus off me and having to explain what I'm doing out here alone. "Where's your group?"

"They're up ahead a little ways. I told 'em I'd catch up.

Just wanted a little time to myself."

I nod, understanding. "Ah. I'll let you be then," I say, and I move to take another step.

"No, it's okay," he says. "We can go together. I could use the company."

I give him a confused look.

"I've been here for a little while. Had enough alone time."

He smiles again, and all of a sudden I feel self-conscious. He was probably here long enough to watch me struggle all the way up this damn pass. He holds out the poles again. "You sure you don't wanna try these? They'll change your world."

There's a note of empathy in his voice, and now I know he was witness to my less-than-adept mountain climbing skills. "Are you sure?" I ask. "Don't you want them?"

"Nah," he says, waving a hand. "I'll be all right." He nudges them at me again, and I take the poles.

"Thank you."

"My pleasure."

There's a moment where neither one of us moves, and I pray that he goes first, but then he puts one hand on his chest and half bows, gesturing with the other.

"After you," he says with a smile.

"Oh no, that's okay," I say. "You go first. I don't want to slow you down."

He picks up his pack and slips his arms through the straps then stands there with a wry smile. "I'm not in a hurry. Go ahead."

He doesn't look like he plans on going anywhere until I do, so I turn and start trudging again. Up the steepest part of the mountain. In front of him.

I move at a pace faster than is comfortable, doing everything I can not to embarrass myself or slow him down. The poles really do make a world of difference, and I can feel we're moving much quicker than I was before, even though the trail is practically vertical. We don't talk, we just move forward. And like many other things out here on the trail, it feels normal, as opposed to real life, where walking with a complete stranger in silence like this would be awkward. I can hear his footsteps behind me, and the only thing that keeps me from glancing back over my shoulder is that I know I wouldn't be able to see past my pack anyway.

I conjure his face in my mind instead. He's cute. Dark wavy hair held back by a bandanna. Warm brown eyes. Kind smile. Broad shoulders that carry his pack with seemingly little effort. For a second, I try to picture what I must look like right now, but I realize just as quickly that I don't have the energy to care. My lungs feel like they're about to burst, and the muscles in my legs and butt burn from deep inside with the effort of the climb. But I can't let up, not with him right behind me and the crest of the pass in my view.

"Wow," he says, just as out of breath as I am, "who are . . . you racing?"

I laugh, but it comes out more like a heavy exhale. "Not racing. I just . . . wanna get . . ." I take two more steps then stop at what looks like the peak. "Here," I say.

Josh stops too, and we both stand there, both try to catch our breath. I look out over the mountain I've just climbed. My first big pass of the hike, and I almost can't believe I made it. I reach back and dig my phone out of the side pocket to get a shot of the view. And then I aim the lens down at Bri's boots and take a picture of them too.

Josh, who's been admiring the view, glances over at me right at that moment. "You want me to get a picture of you?"

"No," I say quickly. "No, thanks."

He shrugs, and I put my phone away. We're both quiet a moment, and this time it does start to feel a little awkward.

"These helped a lot," I say, lifting the trekking poles into the air. "Thank you." I hold them out to him, but he brushes them away.

"Hang on to 'em, if you want." He stands and points at the vast expanse of snow ahead. "They'll be good for that too."

I run my eyes over the seemingly endless peaks and valleys in front of us, trying to hide the sinking feeling in my chest that quickly replaces the previous moment's triumph. "I can't . . ."

What I want to say is that I can't do this. I can't keep going in the snow like this and pretend like it's no big deal. But I bite back the words, feeling embarrassed and weak, and wishing I was alone, with no one else to witness it. I look at Josh. "I can't take these from you. I should've brought my own, and you need to meet up with your friends, and . . ." I try to hand him the poles "Anyway, thank you. They were a big help."

He looks at them, but doesn't take them from me. "Wow. Okay. I can take a hint," he says with a little laugh. "I'll be on my way in just a minute."

"I . . ." I'm trying to give him an out.

"I mean, that's fine if you'd rather go solo, I just thought . . . this part sucks—maybe too much to do alone?"

He pauses, and I get the feeling he might actually be worried about leaving me on my own. I can't decide if that would be endearing or patronizing, but all of a sudden the miles in front of us do look like they'd be a heck of a lot easier with someone else.

I can feel Josh's eyes on me, following my own gaze. "Totally up to you," he says. "And you can keep the poles either way."

I look at him and decide his concern and offer are both genuine. And kind of sweet. "Let's go together then," I say. "At least until it sucks less."

He laughs. "Deal."

We take a couple of minutes to rest and hydrate then we get back to it. Almost immediately, it does start to suck less—partly because we get to start descending, which is such a relief I don't even mind that we have to take switchbacks to do it. But also because it feels good not to be alone. To be in this with another person, even though we don't know each other. We don't talk much as we go—we're connected by a common goal and making progress, and the silence of that is a comfortable one. Thin as it is, it's a connection that feels real, as opposed to so many others I've had.

My mind drifts back to Ian, and how I couldn't believe when he started following me, then started liking and even commenting on my photos. At first I thought maybe it was just a bot set to auto-follow and comment. He had a much bigger following than I did, and he was so good-looking, and so popular, I couldn't believe he'd actually noticed me. And then, when he'd reached out about doing a few paid shots together, I was hopeful that it was an excuse to ask me to hang out. That something in my pictures had intrigued him and he wanted to know more about me. I convinced myself of it, really, so that when we started promoting things and posting as a "couple," I even believed it was true, and that it was me he was interested in. Not the followers or reach I could bring to the table. But for him, it was never about me, or us. Not like that.

Up ahead, Josh stops and waves—I can't see at what, but I assume it's his friends. He turns back then to check on me, and in that one small gesture is more concern and connection than I ever felt from Ian. Not that I expect or want anything to come of it, it's just been nice to be with another person for a little while. I've already decided that once we catch up to his group, I'll bow out and let them go on without me. I don't want to be the one girl in a group of guys, and definitely don't want anyone to feel like they have to look after me. Plus, part of me has gotten used to the idea of doing this thing alone, and being in my own headspace, hiking my own hike, like Corrie said. I try to figure out how to graciously communicate this to Josh as I close the distance between the two of us.

"Be down in a sec!" he yells just before I reach him, and I see I was right. His friends are a few switchbacks below, and when I stop next to Josh and they see me, I hear a "No way!" and whistle, thereby confirming the rightness of my decision to go it alone from this point forward.

Josh glances at me. "Don't worry about them, they're just happy to see me."

There's another eruption of cheers and hoots and hollers from below. "Come on! Do it! Do the Ass Pass!"

I have no idea what they're talking about, so I don't know whether to laugh or be offended. "What did they say?"

Josh shakes his head then laughs a little. "See that trail?" he says, pointing to a smooth line that cuts straight down through the snowy mountainside.

I nod.

"That's from where they slid down the mountain. It's actually called glissading, but we made up our own name for it."

"COME ON!" yells a voice from below. "GO! GO! GO!"

Josh ignores it. "You wanna try? It's quicker than switch-backs, and way more fun."

"I don't . . ."

"It looks kinda sketchy, I know."

"Yeah . . ."

"I'll go first. I can show you how to do it, then you can try." He sits down on his butt at the top of the "slide" and looks up at me before I can argue. "See you at the bottom?"

"Um, sure," I say, though I'm thinking this is the perfect time to part ways as he's about to go barreling down, and I don't want to have to follow.

He tucks the jacket that is tied around his waist under his

butt, sticks his boots with their spiky crampons out in the air in front of him, and leans back slightly. "All right. Wish me luck."

Before I can, he gives himself a shove and is off, sliding down the mountain, slowly at first, and then picking up speed as he crosses right over the first switchback. He yells, and is answered by cheers from below, and he looks so silly bumping down the slide with his backpack, completely out of control, I can't help but laugh.

A few seconds later, he skids to the bottom, and his friends all raise their hands, cheering. As he stands up and dusts himself off, there are high fives all around, and I forget I'm standing there watching it all until they turn their attention up the mountain to me. I curse myself for not having started walking already.

"SEE?" Josh yells. "IT'S SAFE! COME ON DOWN!"

His friends stay quiet, but they're all looking up at me. One of them nudges the one standing next to him.

Shit.

It was one thing to watch him slide down, but going myself is a whole other matter. I glance down at the snow slide, which looks well packed and slick. For a moment, I see myself, careening out of control down the mountain, and landing in a pile in front of Josh and his friends. Who, at this moment, all happen to be looking up, waiting patiently for me to take the slide. I want to yell down

"Thanks anyway!" and keep walking, but a thought stops me then.

Bri would go.

I know it's true. Of course Bri would do this. Not only would she slide down the mountain, it probably would've been her idea in the first place.

I look at the sky like maybe she's watching all this from somewhere up there. *Okay,* I tell her, *keep me safe, and don't let me humiliate myself in front of all those guys down there. Deal?*

I answer for her, then take a deep breath, tuck my jacket beneath my butt like Josh did, and sit with the trekking poles across my lap. Then I give myself a shove. At first I move slowly, but then, just like I watched Josh do, I start to gain speed.

It's a scary, out-of-control rush, and I want to put my feet down like brakes, but in a few seconds I'm moving too fast for that. The only thing I can do is go with it. I hit a bump and let out a little scream without meaning to, but by the time I slide into the flat part at the bottom, I'm laughing and out of breath.

Josh is right there, extending a hand. *"Nice.* I give that an eight for style."

I take his hand and stand, brushing off my pants and jacket.

A stocky guy with blond hair and tattoos covering his arms looks me over, then bumps shoulders with the tall guy next to him and says, not so under his breath. "Dude. I give that a ten."

The tall one laughs but shakes his head. "Shut up, jackass."

"What?" says the tattooed one. "Only Josh would find a cute chick miles from civilization."

I'm surprised when a girl's voice chimes in from behind them. "You guys realize if I can hear you, she can too, right?"

"What?" the tattooed one asks again. "I meant that as a compliment."

The girl stands from where she'd been crouching and gives him a look. "I'm sure you did." She fixes him with her eyes a moment longer until he looks back at me and extends his hand.

"I'm sorry. Name's Beau. Nice to meet you. I just meant you tackled the Ass Pass like a pro." The girl smacks him and he grins, which makes him look instantly boyish.

I shake his hand. "Mari. Thank you—I think."

The girl extends her hand. "I'm Vanessa." We shake, and then she gestures at the other two guys. "This is my boy-friend, Jack," she says, resting her hand on the shoulder of a large-framed guy with brown hair. "And that's Colin." Each of them steps forward, offering polite smiles along with their handshakes.

"That pass was no joke, huh?" Vanessa says when we're finished.

I glance back up the mountain. "Yeah, that was brutal."

"Horrible," Jack says.

"Worst part yet," Colin agrees.

Vanessa nods. "At least it's over, though."

Josh laughs. "That's only the first pass, you guys." He pauses, and glances at me. "The real fun hasn't even begun."

"Are you guys doing the whole John Muir Trail too?" I ask.

"We are. Just like you."

Vanessa looks at me. "Are you hiking *solo*?"

I nod. "Yeah."

"Wow, that's . . . I don't think I could do that," she says.

"I don't know if I can either," I say honestly. Today was harder than anything I've ever done, and if this is just the beginning, I'm screwed.

"But you've gotten this far already," Vanessa says. "That's pretty damn good."

"I don't know," I say quietly. "It doesn't feel like it's that good. I've been hiking so slow, because I'm so sore."

"How far are you going today?"

"I was hoping to make it to Thousand Island Lake by sunset, but I don't know if that's gonna happen." I look at the sun, which peaked in the sky a long time ago and is now beginning its downward arc. "That took a lot longer than I thought it would."

"We'll make it," Josh says. "If we go soon, and pick up our pace from here on out."

His friends all give him a look, and I'm pretty sure I catch a we-never-discussed-this vibe. "What?" he asks, unfazed. "That's where we're going too. It's a good place to camp." He looks at me. "You wanna join us?"

The invitation catches me off guard, even though a tiny part of me had started to hope for one.

"Join you? Oh, I don't—you guys don't need to—" God, I am making this awkward. I pause then look at his friends, who I still can't really read. "I mean, only if it'd be okay with you all—I don't want to intrude on your . . . group." It's the truth, but I also can't really figure a way out of it since we're all headed in the same direction.

Vanessa saves me from embarrassing myself any further. "Of course. Come. Please. We could use a little more estrogen on this trip."

She shoots a look over her shoulder perfectly timed for Colin to tackle Beau in the snow. Jack immediately joins in, firing snowballs at the two of them.

"You see what I mean?" Vanessa says with an eye roll.

I nod, laughing. "Yeah, I just . . . Are you sure?"

"Yes," Vanessa says. "Come. The more the merrier."

Josh catches my eye then and gives me the same wry

smile he did up at the top of the pass. This time it sends a little zing to my stomach that I try to ignore. Doing Bri's hike is what I'm here for. Getting away from my messed-up life and figuring myself out is what I'm here for. Meeting cute guys on the trail is not. I remind myself of this as we get back on the trail, and I have to continue to remind myself as we cover the miles to Thousand Island Lake, with Josh hanging back to match my pace, even though he's very clearly the leader of the group.

RANGE OF LIGHT

WE REACH Thousand Island Lake at dusk, by the light of our headlamps, and it is so beautiful that the exhaustion of the day melts into a quiet kind of awe that settles over us. Without speaking, we all stop to take it in, our reward for the day's efforts.

The sky stretches high above the jagged peaks that surround the lake basin, and the reflections of swirling clouds lit from beneath by the setting sun dance over the surface of the water. True to its name, the lake is dotted with what looks like a thousand tiny islands. All around us, in every direction, a soft light falls on the mountains. It's a deep, warm, rose glow that saturates them so completely it's almost hard to imagine their stony, gray daylight color.

I wish I could capture the image in front of us exactly as it is, press every detail into my memory. The rest of the group stands just a little ahead of Josh and me, and I see that they all have their phones out and are taking pictures. I reach back for my phone to do the same, but when I look at the sky that's changing by the moment, I stop. I don't want to waste a second looking at it through my phone screen. I want to soak up all that light before it disappears. Watch the sun set over the lake, like Bri had planned to do herself.

"Pretty amazing, huh?" Josh says next to me.

I nod without looking at him. "The light . . . it's . . ."

My voice breaks, and I don't have words for the wave of emotion that hits me as I stand there, completely taken with the beauty in front of us. No wonder she wanted to be here for this. It's in this moment that I understand what my aunt Erin meant about finding Bri in nature. I can feel her in this light on the mountains, and the clouds stretched across the twilight sky. Even the breeze is full of something I feel but can't describe.

"Alpenglow," Josh says softly.

"What?" I wipe a tear from my eye, hoping he doesn't notice.

"That light. On the mountains. It's called alpenglow."

I look at him. "Did you just come up with that?"

"No," he says. "I think maybe John Muir did, actually." He gestures at the glowing rose mountains in front of us.

"He was the one who called these mountains the Range of Light."

"What a perfect name," I say.

He smiles. "Yep. I think it's one of those things you have to see for yourself to really understand how awesome it is."

"Yeah," I whisper. "I know what you mean."

I think of how many millions of things there are in the world like that—small, perfect moments just like this that you have to see for yourself to believe and appreciate. Surely more than any one person could see in a lifetime. We stand quiet, watching the alpenglow slip like silk from the mountains as the sun sinks, and I'm sure that Bri saw as many unforgettable moments as she could during hers. I want to keep doing the same.

"Is that why you're out here?" I ask Josh. "To see things like this?"

He thinks about it for a few seconds before answering. "That's a big part of it," he says, glancing down at the ground. I stay quiet, hoping he'll elaborate because I can see in his body language and hear in his voice that there's more.

Instead, he looks at me. "Is that why you are?" he asks.

I think of how when I left, I just wanted to run away from the life I'd created for myself. I didn't give a single thought to what I might find, or see, or discover. And then when I began, I made it about Bri, and honoring her plan.

Now I can see there's so much more to being here—that it's not only about making my way over the miles of the trail that she was supposed to travel, but starting to face up to and sit with the most difficult parts of myself in the process—which is something I'm not ready to talk about right now.

I look at Josh. "Can I get back to you on that? When I figure it out?"

He smiles. "Fair enough."

We watch as Vanessa, Jack, Colin, and Beau make their way down toward the lake to find a camp spot, and I wonder about each of their reasons for being here. For stepping out, and making their way over the trail, day in and day out. For taking on the challenge of doing something out of the ordinary. I fell into it by accident, but each of them chose to do this.

Their silhouettes with their headlamps are dwarfed by the landscape all around, and I have a feeling that's becoming familiar, like we're incredibly small and inconsequential in the face of the towering mountains, but somehow we belong here too. We have a place in all of this wildness.

We find a campsite some distance off from the water. After the tents are pitched, water is pumped, and our nighttime clothes are layered on, Jack, Vanessa, Josh, and I all sit in a tight circle around a lantern, since campfires aren't allowed at this elevation. Beau and Colin have already retired to their tents for that same reason.

Josh sits next to me, the light from his headlamp shining down on the guidebook that details tomorrow's route and destination, which turns out to be the same stop Bri had planned. Not surprising, since it's one of the main resupply stops JMT hikers use. Earlier in the day, we'd all spent a good couple of miles talking about getting there, and fantasizing about what we plan on doing when we arrive, but now we settle in to listen like kids at story time anyway.

He clears his throat. "Ready?"

We nod, and he bows his head again, shining his light onto the pages covered in words and maps. His finger traces the line of the trail.

"Okay, I'm not gonna lie. We've got a long day tomorrow. I'm not even gonna tell you how many miles we're gonna cover. But we're gonna do it because at the end of those miles is a magical place called Red's Meadow Resort." He pauses for effect, then reads in a TV commercial voice: "Where hikers may retrieve food parcels, eat at the café, take a shower, fill water bottles, buy additional supplies, or even sleep in a bed for the night."

We all give a tired cheer.

Jack shoves a forkful of noodles into his mouth. "Man, I wish I was there right now and that this was a burger."

Vanessa twirls a forkful of noodles from the cup in his hand and takes a bite. "Same."

"This time tomorrow night, I'll be three burgers and just as many beers in," Beau says from his tent. He burps like he already is. "Sorry, 'scuse me."

There's the sound of a zipper and Colin pokes his head out of his tent door. "I've been thinking about this all day, you guys. I'm going with one of everything on the menu."

Josh laughs. "Right. You're way too cheap for that."

"No way, not this time," Colin says seriously. "There are some things worth spending your money on, and if this trail has taught me anything, it's that food is one of them. Real food. I'm sick of frickin' granola bars."

I look at the one in my hand, the only thing I could muster enough energy to eat, and I have to agree. Real food sounds like heaven. A shower too. But what I'm most excited about is the little asterisk on the Red's Meadow page of Bri's journal—the one that designates it as a spot for picking up her first resupply box.

Today on the trail, while everyone else was fantasizing about what food the café might have, I was thinking about the box Bri sent herself to receive 59.3 miles into her journey, wondering what might be inside. Just the idea that she packed it herself, like the backpack that I've been carrying, makes me emotional. I try not to get my hopes up too much, but I keep thinking of it like another gift from her. Maybe something that will show me what it is I'm doing out here. And fingers crossed that the box will also have a new supply of Snickers bars.

"So here's what I think we do," Josh says, switching off his headlamp. "Up, eat, and break camp by seven so we hit most of the climbing in the morning, before it gets too hot. We'll take a lunch break at one of the lakes, and then if we make good time, we can hit up Devil's Postpile before we head into Red's Meadow. Sound like a plan?"

A loud snore comes from the boys' tents.

"Yeah, that works," Vanessa says. She grabs Jack's arm. "Come on, babe. Let's get our dishes washed and go to bed."

He nods, and they stand slowly, grimacing at their sore muscles.

"Night, you guys," Josh says.

"Night," they answer together, and then they wander off into the dark, and a few seconds later, Josh and I are alone, with just the light of the lantern between us.

He looks at his watch. "Nine o'clock. Hikers' midnight," he says.

"What does that mean? We turn into pumpkins if we don't go to bed?"

"Pretty much." He yawns and stretches.

"I could fall asleep right here," I say. I'm so exhausted that the walk to my tent seems almost as insurmountable as today's pass.

Josh reaches out and switches the lantern off, leaving a momentary blank space between us. Neither one of us moves or speaks, and in the silence I lean back on my pack and look up at the sky above.

"Wow," I breathe.

"Best part of the day," Josh says.

My eyes adjust, and I can see he's leaned back on his pack like me, head tilted skyward. I look up again, and let my eyes wander over the stars spilled across the night like sparkling dust.

"This is the first time I've seen this since I've been out here."

He sits up a little. "What do you mean?"

"Until today, it's just been me, and I've been so tired I've gone to bed by sunset every night. I haven't seen"—I gesture at the sky—"this." I laugh, embarrassed. "God. I can't believe I haven't seen this."

"It's a good thing you caught up to us then," he says. I can hear the smile in his voice. "You might've made it all the way to Mount Whitney without looking up at the stars."

"And what a shame that would've been," I say.

We both fall quiet, long enough that I wonder if maybe he fell asleep.

"Josh?" I whisper.

"Yeah?"

"Thank you."

"For what?"

"For today. I wouldn't have made it over that pass on my own."

"Yeah, you would've," he says. "Eventually."

I laugh. "Well, I wouldn't have learned about the efficiency of trekking poles, or the Ass Pass, that's for sure."

Now he laughs. "True. You do owe us for that."

"And I'd be holed up in my tent already, missing this again. So thank you—for inviting me to tag along with you guys."

"You're not tagging along with us," he says.

"No? What am I doing then?"

"You're hiking the John Muir Trail. Seeing where it takes you—it's what we're all doing, right?"

I think about it for a minute. "I guess so."

Josh stands. "Good. Then we better get some sleep. So we're ready for wherever it takes us tomorrow."

"Right," I say. "I'll just be out here a little longer."

"Take your time, soak it up."

"I will," I say. "Good night."

"Good night," he answers then disappears into the

darkness. I hear the zipper of his tent open and then close. And then it's quiet again.

I look up at the sky. Imagine Bri somewhere out there, looking back at me. "Thank you for bringing me here," I whisper.

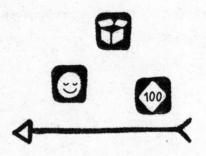

SHADOWS IN THE FOREST

I LIE IN my tent in the morning quiet, looking at today's page in Bri's journal:

I honestly can't wait to wash my spirit—and my entire body—clean. Never in my life have I gone five days without a shower, and while Corrie's methods for rinsing myself and my clothes in the lakes and creeks is something, it's nothing compared to what it will feel like to use soap, and put clean clothes on my clean body.

The rest of the tents are still quiet, so I take the opportunity to slip out of mine before everyone else wakes up. I want to take a picture of Bri's boots here at the lake to mark that they made it like she planned. I slip my feet into the sandals then tiptoe down to the shore carrying Bri's boots. The light is dim, with the sun still hiding behind the mountains, and the air has that fresh smell I look forward to every morning—a mix of everything that's out here—the trees, the wildflowers, and even the dirt. It makes me feel calm and happy as I set the boots at the edge of the perfectly still water. I fish my phone out of my pocket and back up a few steps to make sure I get the mountains and the lake in the background, then crouch down to catch a sliver of the sky too.

"That's a pretty shot," Vanessa's voice says from behind me.

I jump, and spin around to face her. "Oh . . . I was just— I wanted to—"

"Take a picture of your boots by the lake?" she says with a smile. "Artsy. I like it."

I glance at the boots sitting on the shore, and almost tell her that they're not mine, and that I'm not trying to do anything but get a shot of them. But behind her, I see the boys emerging from their tents, and I know now isn't the time.

"Thanks," I say as I scoop them up. "Thought I'd get a picture before we go."

She glances over her shoulder, to where the guys have all sprung into action, rolling up sleeping bags, and breaking down tents. "Better hurry," she says. "Looks like they're raring to go today. Cheeseburgers await."

I smile. "And showers."

"YES!" she says. "Most definitely, showers."

We get packed and moving earlier than I have been on any morning here, motivated by our destination and all that it offers. Our pace is fast, and the trail takes us up. Up through dry hillsides dotted with pale yellow and periwinkle wildflowers. Up beyond one lake, and then down, over sandy switchbacks along another whose shore is lined with tall crimson blooms that I learn are called red paintbrush. They're striking in the morning light. I snap a picture in my mind as we pass them by without stopping.

At the bottom of a thousand-foot descent, we drop back into forest thick with pines and a network of small creeks and streams to cross. There we come across two bearded, middle-aged men coming from the opposite direction. They introduce themselves as Doc and Captain, and after a few minutes of trail talk, we find out they started in Mexico and are thru-hiking all the way up to Canada on the PCT. They tell us about Bear Creek, and how the water's so high they had to use ropes to cross it, and we tell them about the snow in Donohue Pass, and then we wish each other luck and continue on in opposite directions. I'm learning it's what you do out here on the trail, and it surprises me how much I like and look forward to these brief meetings with other hikers. There's a mutual respect and natural cama-raderie there that makes it feel like we're all in it together.

Our group stays together through the flats. I bring up the rear, and have to push to keep up, but the effort gives me something to focus on besides how much my body hurts. It's my blisters that nag at me the most today. This morning, when I realized I was out of bandages, Colin had offered me duct tape to use instead, but I didn't know what to do with it, and couldn't stomach the thought of sticking it to the angry raw skin on my heels, so I'd declined, saying it was no big deal and that I'd be fine. Now that I can feel my socks rubbing and clinging to it, I wish I'd swallowed my pride, asked him what to do, and taken him up on his offer. Lesson learned.

"How you doing back there?" Vanessa asks over her shoulder as we start to climb again.

"Okay," I manage. "You?"

She laughs. "There are three things keeping me moving right now—the prospect of food, a shower, and the ibupro-fen in my resupply box."

"That sounds about right," I say as I almost trip over a

tree root. "Do you guys always keep up this pace?"

She shakes her head. "No, thank god. They're just excited to get there today."

I watch the four heads of the guys bobbing along the trail as they start to pull ahead of us. Every so often one of them laughs or shouts something, and though we're now climbing in earnest, they're clearly enjoying themselves. Which they seem to do no matter what, and it makes the whole thing feel lighter and more fun—a nice change from being so in my own head.

"Have you all been friends for a long time?" I ask Vanessa.

"They have—since elementary school. I met them last year, when I started dating Jack."

"Are you the only girlfriend, or the only one willing to do this with them?" I ask.

We walk a few paces before she answers. "Only girlfriend on the hike," she says. "There was supposed be one more, but she and Josh had a big blowup right before we left, so she bailed."

"Oh," I say. "That's too bad."

We round the corner of a switchback, and Vanessa glances over her shoulder. "Not really. It was for the best, even if he didn't see it at the time."

She doesn't offer anything else, and I don't ask. I don't

want to seem too curious about, or interested in Josh, especially now.

It doesn't surprise me that he had—or maybe still has—a girlfriend. What does surprise me is the tiny sting that I feel at the mention of this. Like I'm somehow jealous of this girl I don't know. And it's not even about Josh. Not really. It's this old, unwelcome feeling, one that I haven't felt out here at all, but it springs back, out of nowhere, and the comparing begins.

I wonder who she is, and if she would've been a better hiker than me, and if she and Vanessa were friends, and if Vanessa wishes she were here instead. I wonder how long she and Josh were together, and if he loved her, and what the fight was about. Whose fault it was, and if it was big enough to break up over. I can't stand that I'm doing it, but I keep going. I wonder what she looks like, and if she's prettier than me. I wonder how many ways the girl a guy like Josh would fall for is better than me.

And then I wonder what is *wrong* with me.

I hate the pit-in-the-stomach, not-good-enough feeling that it gives me to think about all this, but it happens involuntarily, without my permission. A reflex, after years of seeing other girls as competition, constantly trying to measure up, and feeling like I never could.

"So what's your story?" Vanessa asks, interrupting my

crazy-spiral. "Josh said you were supposed to have someone with you, but she had to bow out?"

"Yeah," I say, trying to figure out how to veer away from this topic.

The trail turns us sharply, up the next switchback, and Vanessa catches my eye for a moment. "What happened?"

It's a normal enough question, but my throat goes dry, and my legs feel instantly heavy. I look down at Bri's boots on my feet. "It's complicated," I say, and all of a sudden I want to go back to being alone, and not having to field questions, or worry about what other people might think about the answers.

Ahead of me, Vanessa keeps moving. "Well, for what it's worth, I think it's pretty gutsy for you to be out here on your own. I admire it."

I can't take credit for being gutsy, and there is nothing she should admire about me, but I don't say either of those things. Instead, I slow my pace to try to put some distance between us.

She glances back over her shoulder. "You okay?"

"Yeah, I'm just tired. I think I need to slow down a little—but keep going. I'll catch up with you guys in a bit."

She stops then, and turns to face me. "Are you sure?" She looks concerned, but unsure of how to get around the wall I'm steadily putting up.

I smile. "Positive. Go ahead. I'll catch up."

She nods without saying anything else, then turns and goes slowly around the next bend.

I stay where I am, watching until I can't see her anymore. After a moment, it's just me in the middle of the trail, in the shadows of the forest.

I exhale.

Who am I kidding, letting her think that me being out here on this trail was ever part of my plan? I'm faking it all over again, trying to be something I'm not. Trying to be like Bri. What's worse is that people seem to believe me and I don't have the guts to set them straight and tell them the truth. That I'm only here by accident, fumbling my way through someone else's plan.

I sit down on a fallen tree just a few yards off the trail, and take my pack off. I'm too tired to cry, and the forest doesn't care anyway. It sits silent and impassive, leaving me alone with all these things I don't want to think about as company. Which is probably how it should be. I need to figure out how to separate myself from Vanessa and Josh and everyone else, since I can't bring myself to be honest with them.

Any joy or pride that I've felt over the last few days drains away, and the shade of the forest deepens as a cloud passes in front of the sun. High above me, a breeze moves through the treetops. I can feel a subtle shift in the air, and the sound of a twig snapping makes me jump.

"Hey! There you are," Josh says, coming around a corner. "You okay? We gotta move. Rain's coming."

I look up through the trees at the now dark patches of sky.

"Come on," he says, a little out of breath. "We don't wanna be anywhere near here if there's lightning."

I don't move at first, because I'm so surprised by the fact that I hadn't ever considered what I would do if there were a storm—or the possibility that there could even be one in the middle of summer. Thunder rumbles from somewhere off in the distance, and Josh steps toward me.

"Mari, we need to go. Now."

The urgency in his voice snaps me out of my moment of self-pity, and I get up and put my pack back on. I don't want to, but just like with everything out here, I have no choice. I have to get up and go.

We reach the top of the ridge just in time to see a sheet of rain hanging across the sky a short distance off. Lightning flashes, and I count the seconds in my mind, waiting for the thunder to follow. Josh picks up the pace when it does, a few seconds later. He glances back over his shoulder every few minutes as we start a gradual descent into a barren area that looks like an angry giant came through and knocked all the trees over like dominoes. There is nowhere to take shelter if the storm hits here, so making it through becomes our singular goal.

I don't see the rest of the group anywhere, which means

they must've gone ahead. I'm a little surprised Vanessa did, but she must've sent Josh back for me, like I needed to be rescued or taken care of. I don't like that feeling, but I'm glad he's here. I keep an eye on the sky in front of us and force myself to match his pace so he doesn't feel like he needs to slow down for me. I don't want to be the anchor he's dragging, especially when the rest of the group already went ahead.

After a few steps, I catch up to him. "What do you think happened here?" I ask as we move fast through the surreal landscape of fallen trees.

"A storm," Josh says, above the rising wind. "A few years back."

I look over at the trees toppled like toothpicks across the hillside. "Must've been some storm."

"It was," Josh says. "Hundred and twenty-five mile an hour winds came through here. Knocked down everything for miles."

We push on, and I imagine the angry winds sweeping over the area we're now almost running through. Thunder and lightning and streaks of rain threaten from off in the distance, but it's relatively calm here now. Almost beautiful, in an eerie way. Amid the dead limbs of the fallen trees, there are signs of life I didn't see at first glance. Tiny bits of green that have begun to push their way up through the gnarled trunks and branches.

New growth, after devastation.

I wish I had time to stop and sit in the middle of this place, and soak up the feeling of it. But there's a bright flicker above us, followed immediately by a huge boom that I feel in my chest. Josh and I look at each other, eyes wide as the first few drops of rain start to pelt the dirt around us.

We don't have any other choice but to run.

Our backpacks bounce wildly as the full force of the storm hits, fierce and cold. Lightning flashes directly overhead and sends a jolt of adrenaline through me. Josh must feel it too, because he immediately picks up his pace. Together, we run—faster than I would've thought possible, over the flats, and down into a wide open valley. Racing the rain in the fading afternoon light.

SHE'S NOT HERE

WE SIT INSIDE the Mule House Café, soggy but ecstatic over the feast spread out on the table in front of us. Burgers, sandwiches, shakes, fries, sodas—you name it, we ordered it. The restaurant is packed with hikers seeking warm, hearty meals and refuge from the rain. The staff bustles around cheerfully, serving plates heaped with food that everyone inhales almost as quickly as it appears. A palpable energy dances around the tables of the tiny restaurant, and though we look bedraggled, we are a happy crew.

I take a bite of a thick burger dripping with cheese then wash it down with a gulp of Coke, and it's one of the best things I've ever tasted. I can't eat fast enough, and it makes me feel like some sort of savage, but I don't care. I look around the table, and we're all inhaling our food, manners be damned.

"You guys," Beau says through a mouthful of cheese-burger, "this is the best goddamn thing I've ever tasted."

"Favorite hiking day yet," Colin says.

Jack sets his empty milk shake glass down and reaches for Vanessa's. "Dude, that storm came out of nowhere. That was crazy."

"Hey," she says, reaching for it back. "Not crazy enough for me to let you have my shake too. Here—try this instead." She hands him a piece of pie and slides her chocolate shake back so it's in front of her.

Rain pounds on the windowpane next to us, and I watch the water stream down it, more thankful to be in here with them than pretty much anywhere in my life.

"Man, I'm glad we're here," Josh says, like he can read my thoughts. "Can you imagine being stuck out there in that?"

I take a sip of my own chocolate shake. "No. I would . . . I don't even know what I would do."

Beau reaches for the ketchup bottle. "You'd find some damn shelter and pray you didn't get struck by lightning, that's what you'd do."

"And gear up," Colin says. "You have rain stuff, right?" he asks.

"I . . . um . . ." I don't actually know. "Yeah. I think so,"

I say, trying to sound confident.

"What do you mean, you think so?" Vanessa asks with a laugh. "You packed some, didn't you?"

I play with a straw wrapper on the table. This is a chance to be honest. To tell them about Bri, and this being her backpack, and her trip—all of it. I can lay it out on the table right now, and feel better for telling them the truth. But when I look at their smiling, happy faces, I hesitate. I don't want to make myself and my story the center of their attention.

"I'm sure I did," I say with more confidence. "I just don't remember exactly where I put it. I was gonna go through my stuff later and find it. Make sure I can get to it easy next time."

"Speaking of later, anyone wanna pitch in for a cabin tonight so we don't have to put our tents up in this crap?" Colin asks.

Everyone but me balks.

"Who even are you?" Vanessa asks with a laugh. Then she looks at me. "This guy is the cheapest bastard you'll ever meet."

Colin grins. "I said pitch *in*. It's not too bad if we all split it."

Vanessa whispers something to Jack that makes him laugh. "We're good with our tent," he says.

Beau winks. "I bet you are. Especially after a shower."

She smacks him.

"What? If I had a girl, and we got to get all cleaned up after a week of walking around steeped in hiker funk, that's what I would—"

"Can I get you kids anything else?" Our waitress looks around the table at all of us and smiles.

Our meals have hit us, and we've all slowed down a little on the food. Everyone leans back in their chairs, bellies full and unaccustomed to so much food at once. Jack and Colin have the top buttons of their shorts undone.

"I think we're good here," Josh says. "But where can we pick up our resupply packages?"

"That's gonna be just over there, in that building." She points out the window through the rain, to a line of hikers outside a small redwood building.

"Thank you."

"Sure thing. You best get in line as soon as you can because the office closes at five today, no exceptions."

"Will do, thank you."

She tears our ticket off her book and slides it to the center of the table. "You kids take care. And get here early tomorrow if you wanna beat the breakfast crowd."

"We will," Vanessa says, reaching for the check. "Thank you."

We decide to split the ticket between the six of us, since

we all kind of ordered in a frenzy. Vanessa figures out the tip, and we throw our money in, then head out to get in line for our resupply packages.

Outside, the air is cool and fresh, and the rain has turned into a slight drizzle. The line moves quicker than I expect it to, and soon we're at the front of it. I watch as Jack and Vanessa, Colin and Beau each sign a log and claim their boxes like the prizes they are. Anticipation rises in my chest, and I can hardly believe I was thinking of quitting just a few hours ago. Josh gestures for me to step forward, up to the counter.

"Thanks," I say, trying to suppress a smile.

"Hello," the woman at the counter says. "Name, please?"

"Mari Turner," I answer without thinking.

She scans the list in front of her. "I don't see any Turner here. When did you send it?"

"Oh—I didn't send it, my cousin did. Maybe it's under her name? Bri Young." I start to get nervous as she scans the list again. Maybe Bri never got a chance to send the package.

"Ah," the woman says. "Bri Young." She looks at me, and then over my shoulder. "I'm just going to need Bri, her ID, and signature to claim the package," she says with a smile.

My throat tightens. "She's not here," I say.

The woman purses her lips. "Well, it's her package, so she needs to be here to claim it. I'm sorry, but I can't release it to you."

I try to keep my voice calm. Reasonable, even though it feels harder to breathe all of a sudden. "But I'm her hiking partner. Look." I reach for the crinkled permit that I've kept in the front pocket of her pack since I started, and then smooth it out on the counter in front of the lady for her to examine. I point to my name. "See? Mari Turner. That's me, right there. I can show you my ID too." I take the pack off to dig out my wallet.

"But your name isn't on the package."

The others' conversation trails off as they notice something is off, and I feel Vanessa step up next to me.

"Could we maybe call her?" she asks politely. "She didn't end up making the hike, and—"

The lady takes a big breath and lets it out in a way that communicates her exasperation. "I guess that'd be all right," she says.

"I can't call her," I say, but they don't hear me.

"You can use my phone," Vanessa offers.

I shake my head. "I *can't* call her," I say.

And then I take a deep breath and turn back to the lady behind the counter. "Please. I don't have any way to get in touch with her, but I need this box."

"I'm sorry, darlin', but I cannot give you another hiker's

box without her authorization. That's the rules. No exceptions—except if you want to call her, or have her call us."

I pound my fist down on the counter between us. "YOU DON'T UNDERSTAND! I CAN'T CALL HER!"

Everyone around us goes silent, just as shocked as I am.

"Mari?" Vanessa says softly. She reaches a hand out. "It's okay, we'll figure something out."

"I'm sorry," I say. I take a deep breath and let it out slowly. It's too late to avoid making a scene.

I turn back to the woman behind the counter and speak as calmly as I can. "Bri Young is my cousin. And she's not here because she's dead."

The tears I'd been holding back burst forth.

"Excuse me?" the woman says.

"She died two months ago, training for this hike," I say, my voice thick with tears. "And these are her boots I'm wearing, and her pack I'm carrying, and . . ." I dig in the front pocket for her journal, and when I find it, I hold it up so she can see. "And this says she was going to pick up her first resupply box here. So please. Can I please just do that? She's not coming to get it."

I stand there a moment, breathing hard and wiping my eyes, and then the woman nods slowly. "Of course, sweetheart. I'm so sorry. I'll be right back."

She disappears into a storeroom lined with shelves full of boxes and buckets. I stare straight ahead, silent. I can feel

Vanessa's and everyone else's eyes on me, but I don't turn around. I'm afraid of what I might see if I do.

The woman comes back a few seconds later with a large box. "Here you are. I'm very sorry for your loss."

I sign my name where Bri's should be, then take the package in my arms. "Thank you," I say softly.

And then I turn to walk away and practically run into Vanessa and the rest of the group, who have now gathered behind me as well. They all wear the same stricken look on their faces, and I can tell no one knows what to say.

"I'm sorry," I mumble as I push past them.

Josh reaches his hand out to me. "Mari, wait."

"I can't," I say, brushing him off.

"Let her go," I hear Vanessa say, and they do.

REMEMBER TO LOOK UP

I SIT ALONE in my tent, pocketknife in my hand, staring at the box in front of me. My still-damp clothes cling to my skin, sending chills through me as the evening air cools. Outside the tent, I can hear the jovial voices of other hikers in nearby campsites. I strain a little for any voices that I recognize, but I don't hear them. It's probably best that way. They're probably keeping their distance a few sites away, sitting around a campfire, talking about how they just dodged a bullet by letting me go off on my own.

I open the tiny blade and put the point to the center of the packing tape where Bri's name is written in the same handwriting that's in her journal. I take a deep breath and tell myself that opening this box is what she would want me to do. That, if I want to keep going, I need what's inside.

The tip of the knife pierces the tape, and I drag it down the seam where the box flaps meet, then neatly slice through each end before I open the box. There's a piece of notebook paper folded in half. On it are written the words: *Note to Self.* Beneath them, a swirly, smiley-faced sketch of the sun.

I take the paper out, and though I feel a little guilty about it, open it up to read my cousin's note to herself:

Dear Future Trail Self,

If you're reading this, YOU MADE IT! First 60 miles. Probably wasn't easy, but you're here, and you deserve a treat and a hot shower!

I hope the weather's been good and that you've seen all of the sunrises and sunsets, and slept beneath the stars, and jumped in every lake you passed. I hope the blisters aren't too bad, and that the dehydrated pasta sauce was good - that stuff was expensive.

Mostly I hope you feel completely at home out here on the trail now. I hope that you remember to look up. NOTICE EVERYTHING. TAKE IT IN.

Meet people and make friends, but sit with yourself and your thoughts, and enjoy the alone time too. It's what you came for. You'll never be as free as you are right now, so soak it up. Next box Muir Trail Ranch. Until then, STAY WILD.

♡ Nothing but love, ♡
♡ Bri ♡

P.S. Don't forget to call Mom and check in.

I sit there, holding the letter in my hands. Rain drips from the trees onto the tent in an uneven rhythm. And all I can think is that she should be here. *She* should be here, celebrating making it this far, and feeling proud about a trip full of freedom and adventure, and sunrises and sunsets. Swims in lakes. Sleeping under the stars.

She would've done all of that. But it's me who's here instead.

I've seen a few of the things she mentioned, those quiet moments where the days end or begin. Thanks to the friends I made, I've seen the night sky and the whole universe of stars. And I've certainly spent time alone with my thoughts. Maybe too much. But it seems I'm in for a lot more of that from this point forward after the scene I just made.

I set the letter down and reach for the box. It's filled to the brim, and my trail-mind now notes the weight of each item as I pull it out. On top is a fresh pair of socks, underwear, and a tank top. I press the clothes to my face and breathe in the smell of detergent that immediately reminds me of my aunt's house. Beneath that there is a bag of more bandages and tape, a tube of Neosporin, small bottles containing shampoo and conditioner, soap, and a baggie full of ibuprofen tablets. I pause and swallow three right then, wishing I could share them with Vanessa before I keep going through the box.

Beneath the toiletry layer are a few more basics: an extra set of waterproof matches, more Aquamira drops, wet wipes. Then comes the food, most of it familiar items—oatmeal packets, dried fruit, nuts, jerky, protein bars, peanut butter, pasta with packets of dehydrated sauce. The ever-present ramen noodles. But she threw in a few different items for variety too. There's a box of mac and cheese, a few hot chocolate packets, even some tortillas and salsa. Of course there are the Snickers bars too. At the bottom of the box is an envelope with a twenty-dollar bill inside. I lay it all out on the sleeping bag feeling grateful, and overwhelmed, and a little undeserving of all this.

I reread Bri's note to herself again, all the way through to her P.S.

I know I need to call my mom, that she's probably beside

herself with worry, but the thought of talking to anyone, let alone trying to explain it to her, is exhausting. I don't think I could if I tried. I dig in the pack and pull out my phone, power it on, and now that we're in range of service, watch as the missed call and text notifications register. They're all from my mom and aunt. I swipe the most recent text from my mom open without going back to read all the others. And then I type:

> Hi Mom. I'm so sorry I didn't answer before this. I know you must be worried, but I want you to know that I am safe. And I've decided to hike the whole trail. I just got into Red's Meadow, where I finally have service. I was able to pick up Bri's resupply box, so I'm going to keep going. And I'm not alone. I met a great group of friends to hike with, and we all keep each other safe, so please don't worry. My phone is about to die, but I'll call when we get to our next resupply stop at Muir Trail Ranch, which should be 4 or 5 more days, depending. Please don't worry. This has been good for me, and I'm safe, happy, and with friends. I love you. Mari.

I pause, and glance out the mesh window of my tent. My "friends" are nowhere to be seen, but she doesn't need to know that. After I hit Send, I turn my phone off and tuck it back in my pack, feeling guilty for taking the easy way out with a text, but I'm shivering now, and there's a hot shower waiting. I grab the fresh clothes along with my camp sweats, the little bottle of shampoo and tiny towel, and the twenty-dollar bill and head for the showers.

The hot water is a luxury after rinsing in icy lakes, and the fresh smell of the shampoo and conditioner top it off. But being clean afterward is the best thing about the day. It's dark by the time I get out, and I wish I'd remembered my headlamp, but then I look up at the sky, crystal clear now, so that all the tiny points of light are visible, and I don't mind the dark. It's like the storm and the clouds never even happened. I marvel at how quickly things change out here, and I guess it's the same with me. Today has been an emotional roller coaster, but right now, walking through the campground, with the smell of campfire smoke drifting by, and the little bits of conversation carried along with it, I feel restored.

I wonder, as I walk, where Vanessa and everyone else are, and I decide that after I put my stuff in my tent, I need to find them. At least to apologize for this afternoon and thank them for their company, but let them know that I'm okay going it alone for the rest of the hike. It's the easiest out I can think to give them, and after today, I'm sure they'll take it. I feel a little twinge in my chest at the thought, so I tell myself it'll be good for me to be solo again.

But when I round a curve to where my campsite is, it looks like maybe I won't have to be alone. I first recognize the tents that are set up in a semicircle around mine, and then as I get closer I can see the five of them are gathered around the fire pit, blowing life into a teepee of kindling to start a fire, talking and laughing like they always do.

It puts a lump in my throat, and I stand there a moment, not sure how to approach them.

Beau glances up from the fire and sees me first. "Oh, hey, BA. Hope we're not imposing. Just thought we'd get a fire going."

I walk slowly toward them, still feeling sheepish. "BA?" I ask.

"Yep," Colin says. "We decided that should be your trail name."

"You and Beau decided that," Vanessa says. She looks at me. "Sorry. I didn't get a vote."

"It's a COMPLIMENT," Beau says. He looks at me. "It stands for Badass. Which is what we think you are, for being out here, doing this whole hike to honor your cousin." His voice softens. "It's pretty awesome, you know?"

"That's not . . . I don't think you understand—"

Colin stands and puts a hand on my shoulder. "I think it says somewhere in the hiker's rules that you don't get to argue when someone gives you your trail name. You just gotta accept it."

Everyone else looks at me, their faces sympathetic in the firelight.

I force a smile. "Thank you, really. But I need to explain . . ."

Josh catches my eye. "No you don't," he says gently.

Vanessa takes a step toward me, arms out for a hug. "He's right. You don't need to explain or apologize. Everyone out here has things they're dealing with."

She wraps her arms around my shoulders, and I hug her back. Then it's quiet a moment, like no one knows what to say next.

"Yeah," Colin says solemnly. "I've been dealing with some serious digestive issues since dinner."

Jack waves his hand in the air, like he's clearing it. "Dude. We know."

Vanessa rolls her eyes and then looks at me. "You know what I mean."

I smile. "I do."

Beau comes up and wraps a heavy arm around each of our shoulders. "So are we all good? Because I have a little something to toast with if we are."

I glance at Josh again, and he nods. "We're good."

And just like that, they move on.

Jack and Vanessa grab two pans of Jiffy Pop they bought in the store. Beau proudly produces a bottle of Fireball from his resupply box, while Colin walks around to each of us, gathering our camp mugs. I go back to my tent and grab the hot chocolate packets and the whole bag of candy bars to contribute. It feels like a small gesture after the way they've just forgiven my behavior and rallied around me, but they seem to appreciate it.

We sit around the fire, sipping our cinnamon-spiked hot chocolate, and I listen as they trade funny stories and laugh and talk in the easy way friends do—or that I've imagined they do. For the last few years, I isolated myself from anyone I might've been friends with in real life. I chose strangers instead, because at the end of the day, they could never get too close or see more of me and my life than I wanted to show them.

But today, I didn't get to control what this group saw. They caught a little glimpse of the truth, and based on what they found out about Bri, they decided I'm brave for being out here, and that it's admirable, what I'm doing. And sitting here with them in the fire's fading glow, I wish those things were true. Or that I'd had the courage to tell them they're not.

But it feels like it's too late, and now I don't want them to know—because the whole truth of why I'm out here is more complicated than that.

And infinitely less admirable.

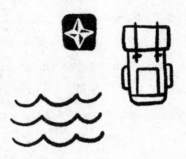

INVISIBLE WEIGHTS

I LIE IN my sleeping bag, listening to the birds outside and watching the sky lighten through the mesh window above me. Our camp is still quiet, which isn't surprising after last night. We stayed up well past hiker's midnight, and I have a feeling it's going to be a slow-moving morning. I'm already dreading getting back on the trail.

I reach for Bri's journal, and flip to the page marked by the ribbon to see what she had in mind for today:

SUNSET SWIM IN PURPLE LAKE

I don't know how far that is, and I don't want to think about it just yet so I set the journal down and pick up my phone instead. The screen lights up, and I stare at the dots that mean I actually have a connection. I've gotten so used to not having it that I almost wish I didn't. There are multiple replies from my mom to the text I sent last night, but again, I don't read them. I already feel guilty about not actually calling her, but I'm afraid that if I did, I'd let her talk me into coming home instead of continuing on. And I'm not ready to go back to whatever is waiting there for me. Not yet.

For a moment, it's tempting to check up on myself—to see what, if anything, is being said about me, or if I'm already long forgotten. But I don't. Instead, I open the Instagram icon and go to Bri's account, because it's her I want to see right now. I stare, for a moment, at the last picture she posted, and it hits me square in the chest that that's it. There won't ever be another photo that comes after this one. Her story ends right when it was really beginning.

Right now I'd give anything to be able to see the next chapter. I know from my mom, and from some of Bri's posts, that she had big plans for after the hike. She'd joined an outdoor education program for girls that would bring her around the world as a mentor for the next two years. Thinking of all the things she would've experienced and lives she would've touched that way makes me sad, so I scroll back in time because that's the only way I can go.

I go through her last months in reverse—her hitchhiking trip to Canada, beyond the beaches of Tenerife, all the way back to the time she spent in Italy, and there's a photo there that catches my eye. It's of her, smiling up at the camera looking calm and happy, holding a basketful of something she's collected. I tap it and read the caption:

> I think this is what I'm going to miss the most about the Italian countryside. I spent this morning picking and collecting walnuts and chestnuts. I'm not really quite sure how to explain what I felt, but I was probably the most relaxed and happy I have been in a long time. There were no noisy cars or planes, just the sound of wind blowing through the trees and birds chirping and the occasional cat that stopped by looking for some attention. My thoughts were so clear it was like I was hearing them for the first time. I have finally started to take the time to get to know myself and just enjoy being in my own presence. I didn't feel the pressure to do anything or think anything, I could just be.

I look at her words, and somehow they soften the edges around the sadness that sits in my chest. Her life was full, if not complete. She experienced big moments, and small ones, and everything in between, and somehow it makes me feel better that she got to experience the particular moment she captured here. It makes me think of the first day I left, and what the lady with the little girl said about how going out is really going in. I wonder if that's what Bri was hoping to do out here on the trail—to get back to that quiet place of being at peace within herself before she went out into the world to lead others to it.

She's already helped me find glimpses of it.

But I want to find more.

So as much as I don't want to get up, or put my hiking clothes on, or get ready for another day on the trail, that's what I do. Before I put her boots on, I walk them over to the campfire ring where we sat last night, and snap a photo of them beside it. She may not be able to add to her story, but I can.

We have a big but quiet breakfast at the café, break camp, then leave Red's Meadow Resort laden down with full packs and a plan to carry them thirteen miles to Purple Lake. We move much slower than we did yesterday, when we had the resort to look forward to. Now, it'll be another fifty miles before our next resupply stop. So between the new weight in our packs, the overcast sky, and the leftover haze that everyone seems to feel from the spiked hot chocolates, morale is low when we take the short junction back to the main trail.

No one talks as we begin the first climb of the day, up toward Crater Creek, and soon enough we have our first creek crossing too. There are enough fallen trees here that we don't have to wade across, so that, at least, is a relief.

Next, the trail takes us up a ravine, over a short pass, and through wet meadowlands. We trudge on silently, each in our own way trying to get our heads back in the trail game after our brief taste of civilization and the comforts that came along with it. It's back to the work of putting one foot in front of the other until we reach our next destination.

This section of the trail is pretty, but kind of monotonous. There are no towering granite domes or cascading waterfalls like in Yosemite that inspired that awed kind of hiking where you pay more attention to the landscape than your aching body. I shared the Advil all around this morning, and that seems to have helped with most aches and pains, but the new weight of my pack rubs uncomfortably on the raw skin of my shoulders and hips, and I'm sure I'm not the only one feeling like we're in for a long day with little reward at the end.

Soon, our group starts to spread out, with Josh and Beau pulling ahead, out of sight. Jack, Colin, Vanessa, and I crunch our way over the dry pumice trail at a slower pace, heading up to begin the steep, switchbacking ascent of Duck Pass. The clouds hang low and gray in the sky, and I eye them warily after yesterday's storm.

"I'm not feeling this today," Colin says. He stops in the middle of the trail, and the three of us who are behind him run into each other.

"You can't just *stop* like that," Jack snaps. "Go to the back if you're gonna pull that stuff."

Colin gives him an irritated look and turns and takes a few steps forward instead, so we start to as well, but then he purposely stops short and Jack crashes into him again.

"What the *hell*?" Jack asks.

Vanessa, who is standing between them and me, rolls her eyes. "Come on, you guys. Don't even get started. Let's go."

Neither one of them moves. They just stand there glaring at each other—long enough that I get worried one of them might throw a punch or something. Vanessa is unfazed by their stare down, but irritated enough to step around them both and keep going, which leaves the two of them and me. I want to go with her, but I'm not comfortable enough to do what she just did. I try to think of something, anything to say to cut the tension.

"Colin—hey. I forgot to tell you, I came up with a trail name for you last night before I fell asleep."

This seems to get his attention. "Oh yeah?" he asks, giving me a side glance.

"I mean it's kind of silly . . ."

Now they both look at me, and it seems ridiculous, the name I thought of. It sounded better last night in my mind, after my Fireball hot chocolate.

"What is it?" Jack asks. Now he's curious too, and they

seem to have forgotten their out-of-nowhere annoyance with each other.

"Well, I was thinking of how much ramen you eat—and how it comes out perfect every time so I thought . . . What about . . . Master Chef? Top Chef? I don't know . . . those are pretty lame now that I say them out loud."

They're both quiet for a second then Colin breaks into his big, goofy grin and laughs. "Those are super lame, not gonna lie. But I like the sentiment. You can call me Top Chef. TC for short."

Jack laughs too. "That's actually pretty funny, since ramen is the only thing he knows how to cook."

Relief washes over me, and I smile. "Yeah?" I look at Jack. "We'll come up with yours next."

"I got a few ideas for names I could call you," Colin says.

Jack shoots him a look. "I bet you do."

They both laugh, and it seems like, for the most part, whatever was bothering them has passed, so we get moving again. We focus on making our way up the steep switch-backs of the pass. I'm still the slowest of the group so I fall back into my own pace and they pull away until I can only catch glimpses of the backpacks in front of me as they round the corners up ahead. Every time I see one of their packs, I think about what Vanessa said the night before, about how everyone out here has their own things they're dealing with.

I wonder what each of theirs is. Jack and Vanessa seem like a happy couple. Colin and Beau are the closest set of friends I've ever seen. Beau seems happy no matter what. And Josh, well, he seems happy enough despite the little that I know about his girlfriend problems. I bet I seemed fine too, before I had to tell the lady at the resort about Bri. It's just what everyone does, I guess. We walk around carrying invisible weights, and doing our best to look like everything is okay even when it may not be.

It's what I've been doing for the last handful of years. It's what all my pictures were about—putting my best face on, choosing the things I wanted to show the world, careful to reveal only the parts I wanted it to see. It's easy to do when you have a screen, and filters, and editing abilities standing between you and real life. But when you actually step out into the world, you don't get those options. Life is right there in front of you, and sometimes the only choice is to be real.

And sometimes it surprises you how people react when you do. Last night, I'd expected the group to be done with me after my outburst about Bri, but the opposite had happened. It's hard to put into words, but once they found out about her, it was like some sort of wall came down and I wasn't so much of an outsider anymore. Maybe because they found out something real about me. The problem is that I feel like I've lied by omission. Last night I let them think that Bri was my sole motivation for being here because I was too scared of what they would think of me if they knew the rest.

And now I can't let them find out.

What I can do, though, is try to learn more about each of them. I've never known a group like this, but I like the feeling of being part of it, so I pick up my pace and decide that from this point forward, I will do what I can to make sure I stay that way.

After a brutal section of switchbacks, I catch up with everyone where they've stopped for lunch just off the trail. It's one of those vistas where we should all be oohing and ahhing over the view, but we just kind of sit in weary silence eating our protein bars and trail mix, and I start to get the feeling that either I missed some exchange between them, or that this is reality setting in. Like when you're on a road trip, and all the initial energy and excitement eventually turns to cramped space, stale air, and clashes in music taste.

"How much farther?" Beau asks, shoulders slumped like he doesn't really want to know the answer.

Josh looks around. "Your guess is as good as mine."

"Don't you have the book?"

"Yeah, but it doesn't matter how far it is. You're gonna complain and have an opinion about it no matter what."

An uncomfortable silence follows. I look around, and

everyone is looking at Josh like he's being a jerk, which he kind of is.

Beau nudges Josh with his elbow. "What's your problem? You're being kind of a dick right now."

Josh puts his hands out in a question. "What? All you did for the last five miles was complain. About everything."

"That's what we do when we hike," Beau says. "We bitch about how much it sucks, then we see something awesome and decide it doesn't suck so much, and then we do it again, over and over, until we make camp. Then we start again the next day. It was your genius idea, we're all just going along with it."

Josh gets up. "Nobody said you had to come."

"No," Beau says. "I guess not. I just came because that's what friends do."

Josh unzips the front pocket of his pack, takes the book out, and tosses it on the ground in front of Beau. "Take it," he says, then zips his pack up and hefts it back onto his shoulders. "I'm gonna go. I'll see you guys at the lake."

Everyone is quiet as he turns and we watch him walk away. It's not until he disappears around a corner that any of us speak.

"Wow," Vanessa says. She turns to Beau. "*What* did you say that got him all twisted up like that?"

"Nothing."

Jack, Colin, and Vanessa all give him a look.

"*Nothing*," Beau repeats, but even I can see there's something they all know about that I don't. Something Beau probably brought up.

I keep quiet.

Vanessa's still looking at Beau. "You mentioned Nicole, didn't you?"

Beau doesn't say anything.

"I thought we agreed not to unless he did." She looks at the other guys, and they nod.

Beau shrugs helplessly. "I know, I'm sorry. I just . . . It was just us, and we were moving at a pretty good pace, and he seemed happy, and I just told him it was good that we were out here without her, and that we were glad because she always treated him like such crap."

"You said we were *glad*?"

"No, no, no. Not that we were glad it happened, just that he's better off without her, that's all I meant, but as soon as I said it I could tell he was pissed. I could barely keep up with him after that."

"Oh man," Colin says. "Now you done it."

Jack shakes his head. "We're screwed. For probably like, a couple of days. Nice one, Fireball."

Beau laughs. "You know how much more screwed we woulda been if she'd actually *come*?"

Vanessa tries to hide her smile.

"You know I'm right," Beau says, looking at her. "What was it you always called her? A vapid bi—"

"Never mind," Vanessa says. She looks at me. "You need the whole story. Josh's girlfriend of three years broke up with him right before the trip. Basically, she told him that she was over it, they had no future, and that his best would never be good enough for her."

I wince. "Ouch."

"Yeah, she was pretty awful—none of us liked her, but Josh loved her—at least in the beginning. Then he just kept trying to make her happy until he couldn't anymore."

I nod slowly, not sure what to say.

"Anyway, it was his turn to pick the summer adventure, and I think he had the idea that somehow this trip would bring them closer . . ."

All three of the guys laugh out loud at this. Vanessa ignores them.

"Like if he could get her away from all the superficial stuff she was into and show her something different, that might help. None of us thought it would work, but we were all gonna go along with it because, well, that's what we do."

"What do you mean? What superficial stuff was she into?" I ask.

"Herself," Beau scoffs.

Colin nods. "Yeah. She was one of those girls who thought she was a model because she took a bunch of duck-lipped selfies all the time."

"Oh," I say quietly.

My cheeks grow hot as they go on to describe how wrapped up she was in her appearance, and how much they all hated that every place they went, it was all about photo ops and how cute she looked. How she was supercompetitive with other girls, especially Vanessa. Every word they say and every jab they take feels like it's a jab at me. At who I was, and I can't listen anymore. Part of me wants to stick up for her. Wants to tell them that maybe they don't know the whole story, or maybe she's not as shallow as they think, or maybe she thinks all those same things about herself but doesn't know what to do or how to change. But they're so sure of what they think of her, and now I'm absolutely sure of what not to share with them.

I need to get away, need a little alone time to clear my head, so I pick up my lunch as quietly as I can while they keep talking, zip it into my pack, and then excuse myself.

"Hey, guys," I say, forcing a smile. "I think I'm gonna get a head start before my legs get too stiff. See you out there? I know you'll catch me before the lake."

They nod their various responses, and I turn to go, but before I can, Vanessa stops me.

"Everything okay?" she asks.

"Yeah, I'm good."

"All right. If you catch Josh, don't tell him we told you about all that."

"Of course not," I say.

She gives a little smile. "And maybe try to keep up with him. He seems to like your company. It might actually cheer him up."

I try to ignore the little flip my stomach does when she says it, and I go, but I don't catch up to Josh, and even after a couple of miles, no one catches up to me. It's just as well. It takes about as long to stop replaying everything they were saying about his ex and making it about me instead, and some distance beyond that to find something else to think about.

I stop in the middle of the trail and close my eyes. I try to give myself permission to just be, like Bri wrote about. To not think about anyone else, or what they think of me, but just enjoy being in my own presence, like she said. But that conversation, about Josh's ex, has stirred up too much of my old life and triggered so many insecurities, I can't find my way to that quiet, peaceful place. I open my eyes and take a deep breath and try to send out all the noise from my mind on the exhale.

And then I remember something Bri taught me one summer: three deep breaths.

She'd said that's what made her brave any time she was

scared of something, and so I'd practiced it on our adventures together, any time she led me out of my comfort zone.

I can't believe I forgot, but I'm so glad I remembered.

I take my three deep breaths, and almost immediately, I feel the sun on my skin, and I can hear the birds high in the trees like they just arrived. I notice the bright red and periwinkle splashes of the wildflowers along the trail, and the way the rock has transformed from granite to a darker volcanic rock woven into the mountainside. I start walking again, and soon I find a new place—one without words or thoughts, where I am not so much moving through the landscape, but a part of it.

I thank Bri for that, and then I let myself sink so deep into it that I lose track of time and distance, and even the aches and pains of my body, so it's a surprise when I come up a gentle rise to a mirror-smooth sapphire lake tucked perfectly into the rocky basin. On its shore is a tent I recognize, but I don't see Josh anywhere nearby.

Still marveling that I somehow made it here already, I pick my way down to where the tent is as quietly as I can, just in case he's sleeping inside.

"Hello?" a voice calls in response to my footsteps.

When I reach the tent, I see Josh stretched out on a rock in front of it, shirtless in the sun. He sits up when he sees me, looks over my shoulder for the others, then back at me. "Hi," he says with a smile. "This is unexpected."

"What? That I got here before everyone else?" I take my pack off, smiling at the relief.

He nods. "Yeah. Did they . . . ?"

"They said they were gonna take it slow, and I was feeling good, so I just kept going, and this . . ." I look around at the mountains framing the lake that reflects the sky. "This is so worth it." And then, carefully, I add, "One of those parts that doesn't suck so much."

He laughs. "Yeah. Listen, sorry I was a jerk back there. I just have a lot on my mind, and sometimes Beau knows exactly what buttons to push."

I sit down on the rock next to him. "It's okay. Like Vanessa said, everyone's got their stuff."

He takes a sip from his water bottle and looks around. "Yeah, I guess we do."

We sit there in the quiet you can only find high in the mountains, a silence that feels more profound than anything else, and Josh looks at me like he wants to say something, but just then we hear the familiar voices of the rest of the group coming up the rise behind us. I stand up and wave, and they all come down over the rocks looking ragged and worn.

They take off their packs nearby but don't say much, and I can feel the tension in the air between them and Josh. I watch quietly, curious about who will speak first. None of them do. They all take a few moments to stretch then

Vanessa and Jack pull out their tent and get straight to work putting it up, and Colin and Beau do the same a short distance away.

For a few moments, the only sounds are of nylon and poles snapping together. But then one of them starts humming. It's a song I recognize, but can't place at first. I tune in, realizing that it's Beau. When he sees me looking, he adds the words.

"Blue jean baby, LA lady . . ."

"Here it comes," Colin says with a smile.

Beau walks toward where Josh and I are sitting, singing a little louder now. "Seamstress for the band . . ."

Josh drops his chin to hide his smile and shakes his head. "Don't."

"What?" Beau says, getting even closer. "I totally saw it work in a movie one time." He winks at me.

And then, without warning, he drops to his knees next to Josh and wraps his tattooed arms around him so he can't move. Then he hits the chorus—hard: "Hold me closer, tiny daaancer . . . Count the headlights on the highway . . ."

I can't help but laugh, and neither can Josh.

Beau stops his singing long enough to grab Josh by both sides of his head and pull him in close. "Can I get a little backup here?" He repeats the chorus, then laughs. "Dude, those are the only words I know."

Josh pushes him off, but he's laughing, and now so is

everyone else, except Beau. He rises, his face in serious serenade mode, and keeps singing the chorus, over and over, until Josh finally puts him into a half-headlock, half-hug, and joins in.

And then we all do. There on the shore of Purple Lake, we sing our own little moment of solidarity, and the band is back together.

After, we find a good campsite and get our setup tasks all done, then head down to the rocky shore of the lake to soak our blistered feet in the icy water and wash up a bit before the sun starts to sink and the temperature falls. I take my boots off and set them on the rock next to me, then peel each sock off as gingerly as possible, afraid to look at the day's damage.

I feel it the second I dip my feet in the water, and everyone else does too, judging by the winces and moans as we wade into the lake. After a few seconds, the initial sting of the cold water against raw skin dissipates, and a prickly numbness takes over.

"Ahh, that's nice," Beau says. "Doesn't even feel like I have feet anymore."

"Look how clear it is," Vanessa says, swirling a foot in front of her.

I look down into the blue-green water that's so clear I can see all the way down to the rocky bottom. It almost makes me want to dive in. Then I remember Bri's plan for the day—the one thing on the agenda—and before I can think about it too long, or change my mind, I stand up and dive in, clothes and all.

The cold is electric—a shock to the system—but I hold my breath and glide as far as I can. I hear a muffled splash behind me, and then another and another, and when my head breaks the surface, I see everyone has followed me.

Josh's head pops up out of the water, followed by Vanessa's and the rest of the guys.

"Holy *shit*, that's cold!" Colin yells.

Vanessa squints. "I think I just blacked out for a second."

"You're crazy, BA!" Beau yells.

I laugh. "You didn't have to follow me!"

Josh swims over to where I'm treading water, too cold to catch my breath. He stops right in front of me, close enough that our legs brush beneath the surface. He smiles. "I didn't see that coming," he says.

I push away the tiniest bit, putting a little more space between us. "Neither did I," I say, breathless from the cold. "It was kind of an inspired moment."

"Those are the best kind," he says. And we linger there for a second as the sun begins to sink behind the mountains.

"I almost forgot," I say, making for the shore. "There's something I need to do."

Josh swims after me, and when we reach the shore, I run

to my pack and grab my phone, then scoop up Bri's boots. When I set them on the sandy edge of the lake, one of the boots falls over on its side, but I leave it because the sun is sinking faster by the second, and I want to be sure to capture the light on the water.

I crouch down and snap one, two, three photos just as the sun disappears, and then I sit there a moment, shivering in the evening air.

The sky is a palette of pastels, and when I look up, I spot a single star, already shining.

"We made it," I whisper.

GIRL, BE BRAVE

THE NEXT MORNING, we rise early in preparation for another long mileage day and set about the tasks of filtering water, making breakfast, and then breaking camp as the soft light lifts from the mountains and the day opens up in front of us.

We hit the trail ahead of schedule, all of us happy that the first section is slightly downhill. Soon, we reach Lake Virginia, another small alpine gem surrounded by a meadow bursting with wildflowers. Yellow and red and purple shine bright beneath the cloudless sky, and the day feels full of possibility.

I feel strong today, like I've finally got my trail legs. We pass through another flower-covered meadow and descend down into a canyon along Fish Creek, which is dotted by big slabs of granite that create deep blue swimming holes. The sun is up, and the heat of the day is rising, and though it's tempting to stop and take a dip, we've all agreed to make as many miles as we can today.

We didn't come across any other hikers yesterday, but today we meet two middle-aged men and their wives at our first creek crossing. They're friendly and talkative and after the standard exchange of where each of our parties is headed, they seem surprised that "such young people" are out here, particularly Vanessa and me. One of the wives, a slight woman with short brown hair pulls the two of us aside.

"I so admire you girls for hiking this trail. I wouldn't have thought to do it, let alone been allowed to, when I was your age."

We smile and nod.

"It's just wonderful, just so good to see young women out here doing this. You girls should be proud of yourselves."

Vanessa glances at me before she answers the woman. "Thank you. And we are proud—right, Mari?" She bumps me with her shoulder.

"Right," I say, and it makes me smile.

We're about to part ways when one of the men speaks up. "I wish you guys all the best. And listen, Silver Pass Creek is running high right now. Really high. Usually, there are three boulders you can use to cross, but this year only the tops are showing." He eyes the sandals hanging off our backpacks. "Leave your shoes on for that crossing. The water's turbulent, and the creek bed is rocky. Hard to get your footing if you fall in.

"And be extra careful with your food. Lots of bear activity being reported from all over the trail. They're out and hungry."

"Got it," Josh says. "Will do."

"Thank you, sir," Colin answers.

We say our good-byes, then cross over the bubbling stream on a footbridge and the JMT winds its way deep into a dense forest—the first we've been through for a little while. The trail follows the creek through the thick woods, and we start to climb toward Silver Pass. By the time we reach the top and descend to Silver Pass Lake, it's noon.

After a quick stop for lunch, we're back on the trail, full steam ahead, pushing through the alternating sandy flats and rich green meadows, where two squirrels stand on their hind legs and stare like mini-sentinels as we pass by. When the trail dips back into the forest, it takes on an almost magical quality. Granite slabs push up through the ground again, and clusters of bright, rose-pink flowers dot the crevices between them. We cross Silver Pass Creek a few times, but it's more of a stream at this point, meandering peacefully through a meadow, and I can't help but think that the man had maybe exaggerated about the danger. It's easy to see how it happens—it's much more interesting to tell about a wild river crossing than a bubbling stream in a field of wildflowers.

As soon as I have the thought though, we round a corner and the trees give way to a view of the valley that drops steeply in front of us. To the left, water rushes over a sheer granite cliff in tumbling cascades before it joins the creek below in a frothy explosion of whitewater on rocks. The view is breathtaking and dizzying at the same time. We all stand there a moment, taking it in.

"Wow," I breathe. "It's beautiful."

Vanessa steps up next to me. "It's dangerous," she says, pointing down the slope, past the rocky switchbacks, to where the trail ends at the roiling river. Sure enough, the tops of three boulders peek out from the swirling water.

"Those guys weren't joking," Josh says. "Come on. Let's go check it out."

We get moving again, and I stumble more than once on my way down because I'm not looking where I'm going. I can't take my eyes off the river and the way it rushes and churns around the rocks where we're supposed to cross. My mind goes again to the four hikers the man in the permit office told me about, and I'm sure at least one of them was swept away here. I have a bad feeling about this, and it's made even worse when we get to the crossing and I can see that farther down, the river disappears over another ledge.

We stand at the edge of the creek in one of the calmer stretches, where the water laps gently over the shallow rocky bottom. No one speaks at first, and maybe it's because they're thinking the same thing I am. That this is a bad idea. We should turn around, or try to find another place to cross. We should do anything but this.

I'm about to remind them of what the man in the Wilderness Office said, that nothing out here is worth dying for, when Josh takes one of the trekking poles from his pack, extends it, and takes a few steps into the water, boots and all. I see his muscles tense to hold his footing when the water hits his calves. He plunges the pole into the water at the center to test the depth and current, and holds it there a moment, surveying the other side. Colin, Beau, and Jack join him to do the same. Vanessa and I stay on shore.

"I don't think we should do this," I whisper to her, eyeing the fast-moving current.

Vanessa doesn't take her eyes off Jack as he ventures out farther into the middle of the river, where the water is thigh-high on his six-foot frame.

"If it's not safe, we won't," she says.

That doesn't make me feel any better. I don't know whether to hope that it's safe enough to cross, or so unsafe we have to go off trail and find another route. The boys turn and carefully shuffle their way back to where we are standing.

"It's safe!" Beau calls.

Jack looks at Vanessa. "We can make it."

"Can *we* make it?" she asks. "That water's gonna be almost waist-high on us." I'm not sure if she's asking for both of us, or if she's just trying to be polite while asking about me, who seems to be the weakest link of the group.

Josh nods. "Yeah. We'll partner up and go slow."

"Are you sure?" I ask.

He looks at me. "I'm sure. Here's what we're gonna do."

I try to focus on his words as he describes how we're going to make it to the other side. We'll cross in pairs at an angle, facing upstream and shuffling our feet over the rocky bottom as slowly and carefully as possible, while we hold on to each other for added stability. It makes sense and sounds reasonable until he tells us all to unbuckle our pack straps in case we lose our footing and need to ditch our packs to save ourselves. That's when the only things I hear are the rush of the water, the ranger's words about the hikers who were swept away, and my own heart pounding in my ears.

"I can't do this," I blurt out.

They all look at me. Everyone except Josh looks as nervous and tense as I feel, but they don't say anything.

Josh steps closer so that he's standing right in front of

me. "You can," he says, looking me right in the eye. "We'll go slow, take it one step at a time."

One step.

The words echo in my head. One wrong step was all it took for Bri, and she knew what she was doing. I glance around at everyone else as they prepare to cross—making sure waterproof bags are sealed, tying their shirts up around their waists, checking the laces of their boots, gathering their courage while I stand frozen with fear. I close my eyes and take three deep breaths and try to conjure Bri and her courage, but all I see is myself getting swept down the river, toward the ledge, knowing what's coming.

When I open my eyes, Vanessa is there. She reaches out and puts a firm hand on my shoulder. "Girl, be brave. We'll be okay. Promise."

The icy water seeps into my boots and through my socks almost immediately, and my heart pounds in my chest. I hesitate when I feel the unevenness of the rocky bottom. Josh, whose arm is hooked with mine, stops immediately.

"You okay?"

I nod.

"All right. Here we go. Just like they're doing out there."

I glance toward the middle of the river, where Jack and Vanessa, and Beau and Colin are paired off, doing the same slow sideways shuffle through the fast-moving water.

We continue, and I can feel the force of the current as it swirls around my calves and then my knees, pulling hard, just waiting for a foot to slip so it can grab hold and sweep me under.

"Left," Josh says, and we both slide our left feet. "Right." We do the same with the right, and my legs shake with each step.

The water creeps up over my knees, pushing hard against my legs, which tense in response to the force and the cold. Slowly, we inch our way out into the middle of the creek, and I begin to relax the tiniest bit into the rhythm we've got going. We're making it. Just like we've made it up the snowy mountain passes, and through the rainstorm, and over more miles than I've ever gone in my life. All of these things seemed insurmountable to me before I took a chance and tried them, and now it's the same with this. I glance up and see Beau and Colin hit the shore, followed by Jack and Vanessa, and I smile, thankful for the way being with them all makes me feel braver.

"Left," Josh says. I slide my left foot just like I've done each time he said it. But the second I do, my foot slips down the side of a large rock, and I pitch forward so hard I yank Josh too.

He tenses and plants both of his feet just as my other foot slips out from under me. In an instant, the water takes both of my feet, heavy with the weight of the soaked boots, and sweeps them behind me. I gasp as my knee smacks a rock and my chest hits the icy water. Josh's arm squeezes around mine hard, and yanks upward to keep my face from going under, and the force of it rolls me onto my side. Immediately, I feel the weight of my pack shift and then tip into the creek.

"Hang on!" Josh yells.

I feel the pockets of the pack catch and begin to fill with water.

Josh bends over me and shifts so that his leg braces both of mine. The current pins my legs against his, and I feel him hunker down to fight the pull of the water on my pack, which is getting heavier by the second.

"Hang on," he says again through gritted teeth.

I hear Beau's voice. "Oh shit!"

There's splashing. Jack's and Colin's voices.

"Mari!" Vanessa screams.

Josh's eyes lock on mine. "I got you, okay? Just hang on to me."

I can't breathe or speak, but I nod.

"Your feet," he says. "Can you get them under you?"

I shake my head. My feet are lead weights trying to drag me down the river.

"You have to try," he says. "On the count of three. Dig your feet into the bottom as hard as you can, okay? On the count of three. One . . . two . . . THREE!"

When he says it, he braces and I use all my strength to try to do what he says and dig my heels into the rocky bottom of the creek. One of them catches, and the force flips me onto my back just as Jack, Colin, and Beau reach us. Colin grabs my free arm, and the other two get ahold of my pack, lifting it up so I can get both feet beneath me and stand up again.

Water pours from it when I do, and even with Josh and Colin helping me, the weight is unmanageable.

"Can you guys get the pack?" Josh asks them.

"Yeah. We got it."

Josh looks at me. "You're gonna take it off, okay? One strap at a time. And you're gonna hold on to me as you do it. Got it?"

I nod, still unable to speak, already shivering from the cold.

"Here we go." He helps me with one arm and then the other, and Jack and Beau take the weight of the pack. As soon as I'm free of it, Josh hooks his elbow with mine again and we inch toward the shore, which isn't far off at this point. Colin joins the other guys to help with my soaked pack, and in what seems like just a few steps, we reach the safety of the shore and all of us flop down on the granite slab where Vanessa is waiting.

"Oh my god," she says. "Are you okay?"

I lie on my back, eyes to the blue of the sky and exhale a shaky breath. "I think so."

Josh finds my hand and squeezes. "You sure?"

I turn and look at him lying next to me, cheeks flushed and clothes soaked, and I know I am alive because of him. "Really," I say. "Thank you. That was . . ."

"Pretty damn impressive," Beau says. "Do you know how much this thing weighs right now?"

I sit up and look at where my backpack sits like a soggy monster, water streaming from its pockets, in the middle of Jack, Colin, and Beau.

"You guys are superhuman," I say. "Thank you."

Colin bumps shoulders with Jack. "It was Hulk over here who dragged that thing out."

Jack, who's still out of breath, laughs.

"I think you just earned yourself a trail name," Beau says.

Vanessa kneels behind Jack, slides her arms around his chest, and tucks her chin into the space between his neck and shoulder. "I think you did, Hulk."

Josh gets to his feet and walks over to my backpack so I do the same, despite the pain in my knee. The flow of water from the pack has slowed to a trickle that makes its way down the granite slope to rejoin the creek. I loop my hand through the top strap and pull up to test the weight.

"There's no way," Josh says. "We're gonna have to let it dry out." He looks at the others. "I'll stay back with Mari, if you guys wanna keep going."

Beau smirks.

"You don't have to do that," I say quickly. "I'll be okay. I don't wanna set you guys back any more than I already have. You should all keep going." I try to mean it, but I don't want them to go. I don't want to be alone right now.

"Stop," Vanessa says, glancing from me to Josh. "Both of you. We'll take the afternoon off, stay here tonight, then catch up tomorrow." She looks around at the rest of the group. "Sound good?"

They all nod, and without giving it another thought, spread out to find a good place to make camp.

Josh looks at me and smiles. "I think you're officially part of the crew, whether you want to be or not."

I watch as Jack and Vanessa, and Beau and Colin pick their way over the boulders on the shore, and then I look back at Josh.

"Good," I say. "Because I want to be."

WHAT WE CAME LOOKING FOR

WE FIND A clearing amongst the pines about ten yards away from the creek, complete with a wide, flat expanse of granite. After Josh helps me drag my pack over to it, I get to work unloading and spreading out the contents to assess the damage and let things start to dry out on the rocks in the midday sun.

As it turns out, bear canisters are not only bear-proof, but waterproof as well, so the bulk of my food is safe. Most everything aside from my sleeping bag, tent, and clothes is packaged up in the Ziploc bags, the way Bri had originally sent them, so those things are safe too. All in all, I count myself extremely lucky—not just to have my life and my pack, but not to have lost anything to my unintentional dip in the creek.

And then I spot Bri's journal.

It's still there in the pack, but when I take it out, and see that the leather on the outside is completely saturated, my stomach drops. I sit down and cradle it in my lap, hoping the pages with her writing were somehow spared, and that the water didn't make it all the way through.

But when I open it, all I see is watery, blurred ink.

I feel Josh watching me as I turn the wet pages, hoping that something, anything is left.

"Your journal?" he asks quietly.

At first I nod. Then I shake my head.

"No. My cousin's."

"Oh no."

The note of sympathy in his voice releases the tears I've been holding back since he dragged me out of the water.

"Maybe we can save it," he says quickly. "Let it dry out in the sun with the rest of your things?"

"I don't think so," I say, looking down at it. I wipe at my eyes and try to tell myself things could've been much worse. I could've lost everything. I could've been swept down the river like those other hikers, but this feels almost as tragic. I look at Josh.

"It had her plans in it—for this trip—these daily things

I was following, and now . . ." I look down at the blurry words on a page I hadn't even gotten a chance to read yet.

"You asked the other day why I was out here," I say. "It's because of her. When we were kids, we talked about doing this hike together when we turned eighteen, but things changed, and when she—" I pause, and bite my lip. "We weren't close anymore when she died, but I thought coming out here with her things and her plans might somehow help me find . . ." I shake my head. "I don't know. It doesn't really make sense, but . . ."

"It makes perfect sense," Josh says, and there's something in his tone that makes me believe he really thinks so.

He's quiet a moment, then he looks at me. "A few days ago, you asked me why I'm out here."

He gets up and goes to his backpack, unzips it, and pulls something out. When he comes back and sits down, he's holding a Ziploc baggie with a picture of a guy who looks just like him, dressed in old school–looking hiking clothes, standing on an impossibly tall rock ledge high above what looks like Yosemite Valley.

"This is my dad," he says. "He did this hike with his best friend when they graduated from high school, and he said it was one of the best experiences of his life." He looks down at the picture. "It was right after my mom told him she was pregnant with me. He said all he'd wanted to do when he found out was escape because he wasn't ready to be a dad, or a husband. So he left, thinking he might not ever come back. But by the time he made it to Mount Whitney, everything had changed. He'd had enough time to figure out what he wanted, and he couldn't get down that mountain fast enough to tell my mom it was a life with her—and me."

I smile. "I love that."

"Yeah," he says. "Me too. It worked out pretty good for all of us."

We both look down at the photo of his dad. Josh shrugs. "Anyway, I guess I was hoping I might figure out what I want, like he did."

"Have you?" I ask.

He laughs. "Not really. I guess I've more figured out what I *don't* want."

"What don't you want, then?"

"Hm." He takes in a deep breath and lets it out slowly. "Well, I definitely *don't* want to go home and get back together with the girl I was dating," he says.

We both laugh, and he shakes his head. "That's a long story, with lots of good, hard-earned life lessons at the end."

He picks up a pebble and tosses it into the middle of the creek, and neither of us says anything as we watch the water flow over the spot where it disappears.

He takes another deep breath.

"I guess mainly, I don't want to have one of those ordinary lives that no one plans on having, but most people end up with," he says. "And I don't want to forget what it feels like to be out here like this—so I want to keep doing things that remind me."

He pauses. Looks at me. And then a slow smile spreads over his face.

"And now you know all my secrets. It's that damn trail phenomenon that happens, where you tell people things you never would in real life."

I laugh. "Is that what it is?"

Josh nods. "Most definitely. Anyway," he says. "As long as we're being philosophical . . . I don't think that what we came looking for is as important as what we end up finding out here."

I look at him, then back out at the creek, and think about what I've found so far. What I'm *finding*, every day I spend on the trail—strength and gratitude and wonder—all of these things I didn't start out looking for.

"Thank you," I say. I reach out and take his hand in mine, and we sit for a few minutes in the silence and the sunlight of a place that feels like ours alone.

But, like always, the trail has a way of bringing you back to the present moment no matter what, and in the back of my mind, I know that there are only so many hours of sun left, and that I have to deal with the rest of my stuff if there's going to be any chance of it drying before nightfall.

Josh helps me out with my tent, and we put it up to dry even though it sags with the dampness still in the fabric. My sleeping bag is trickier and takes longer, but Colin figures out a way to hang it from a tree, propped open with a few of the trekking poles, and I hope it'll be okay by bedtime. Next, I work on the rest of my things that got wet—clothes, boots, and everything else—I spread it all out on the warm granite to soak up the sun.

I grab the pack to do the same, and that's when I see Bri's dreamcatcher still attached to one of the zippers, which feels like a small miracle after my plunge into the river. I reach for it, and my eyes well up when I take its sunflower center in my hand. The thin leather cords that hang from the bottom are tangled and damp, but it's otherwise intact.

Carefully, I take it off the pack and lay it down on the rock in front of me so I can untangle the cords. At the end of each one is a small bead that represents one of the four elements—a leaf for earth, a feather for air, a shell for water, and a star for fire. As I lay each one out, I see us—sitting on her porch at the edge of the meadow, my matching dream-catcher in my hand, and Bri explaining how it would guide me where I needed to go and protect me along the way.

And now hers is right here, doing exactly that.

I pick it up and press it to my chest, then lay back against the warm rock and whisper my thank-you to the sky.

For the rest of the day, we lounge in the sun, wade in the water, and make the most of our unexpected afternoon of rest. After dinner, we sit huddled around a crackling fire, sipping hot chocolate, still surrounded by the entire contents of my backpack laid out on the rocks all around.

"I'm beat," Colin says as he stretches in the dying firelight. "I gotta hit the sack."

Beau yawns. "Right behind you, honey."

They both get up and hobble to their tents, arms around each other for support, and disappear without another word. Vanessa looks over at Jack. "You ready, babe?"

He nods, and they do the same, and then it's just me and Josh and the smoldering embers in front of us.

He looks over at me. "I can stay up with this until it goes out if you wanna turn in too."

I glance at the silhouette of my sleeping bag hanging from the tree, and shiver despite the fact that I'm bundled in a mix of everyone else's clothes. There's no way it's going to be dry by now.

"I might just sleep out here by the fire," I say, curling my hands around my mug like it'll help keep me warm.

"Oh. Yeah," Josh says, following my eyes. "I forgot about

that." He clears his throat. "Um. You can share mine if you want."

I almost choke on my hot chocolate. "Share your *sleeping bag?*"

There's a snicker from the boys' tents, and then a hush I know is Vanessa, and I wonder for a second if their whole "I'm tired" thing was a calculated act to land us alone, next to the dying fire, with one dry sleeping bag between the two of us.

Josh shrugs. "Or you can just have it for the night."

"What would you do then? I can't take your sleeping bag."

"SHARE IT!" Beau calls from his tent.

That makes them all laugh, and in the quiet that follows, I can sense them waiting to hear what I'll say to that. My stomach flutters at the image of Josh and me tucked into his sleeping bag.

I get up and check mine, but it's still damp. And now cold. I would freeze overnight if I tried to sleep in it. I tell myself it's no big deal. That we probably wouldn't be the first hikers who had to share a sleeping bag temporarily. Out of necessity. I look around at our tents all pitched in close proximity, and then my eyes find the slope of granite on the opposite side, and I remember something Bri mentioned in her letter from the resupply box. One of the things I haven't done yet.

"Can we sleep under the stars?" I ask.

Josh looks surprised. "Really?"

"Really. It's so clear tonight, I think we should."

He grins. "I like your style. I think we should too."

It only takes us a minute to gather up his sleeping mat and pillow, which he hands me. "Here. You can use this."

Before I can argue, he grabs a sweatshirt from his pack, rolls it up, and tucks it under his arm. We head away from the tents, over to the rock, and find the flattest part to make our bed for the night. Once it's all laid out, we stand there a moment—hesitating, because the next thing to do is crawl in together. It's dark. New-moon dark, and it takes a few seconds for my eyes to adjust, but then I can see the outline of Josh's body against the silhouettes of the trees.

"This is okay here, right?" he asks.

I look up at the stars spilled across the night sky. "Perfect."

"Go ahead," he says, gesturing down at the makeshift bed between us. "You first."

"Thanks," I say, and I bend over and unzip the sleeping bag, then slide in, acutely aware of how little room there is inside.

Josh sits down and takes off his shoes, then swings his legs into the bag next to mine. It's snug, and there's no getting around the fact that every inch of us, from our ankles on up to our hips is touching. We lie down at the same time, slowly, until we're both flat on our backs, each doing our best to give the other one space. It's the most uncomfortable position for sleeping I can imagine.

"Sorry," I say, trying to scoot as far as I can into the seam on my side. "I don't know if this is gonna work."

Josh laughs and does the same. "It's okay. We can fit. We'll make it work."

We readjust multiple times until we're settled on our backs, rolled shirts beneath our heads, looking up at the sky above us. It's not comfortable, and I don't think I'll actually be able to sleep like this, but it's better than the alternative of my wet sleeping bag. And the view tonight is worth it.

We both go quiet, and I don't know if it's because he's taking it in too, or because he doesn't know what to say. For me, it's both. I realize the last time I slept under the stars was with Bri, during that last summer we spent together, searching the sky every night for shooting stars.

I scan the night, hoping to catch a glimpse of one. After a moment, a movement in the corner of my eye catches my attention. It's a tiny light moving across the sky, but it's too slow to be a shooting star. It doesn't have the blinking lights of an airplane either. I follow its steady pace, trying to figure out what it is, and then it disappears.

"Did you see that?" I ask Josh.

"See what?"

"That tiny light that was moving—like a plane, but not?"

He's quiet for a second. "Like that?" he says, pointing straight up above us.

It takes me a second, but I spot what he's talking about, and it's the same thing. "Yes! Just like that," I say, and I follow its arc again until it disappears.

"Satellites," Josh says. "They're everywhere if you look for them."

"*Really?* Like *space* satellites?" I scan the sky for more.

He laughs. "I don't know if that's the official name, but yeah, I guess so—for cell phones, TV, internet. It's all up there, orbiting around. You can even see the space station when it passes by."

I spot one, and then another as he speaks. "I can't believe we can see them from here."

"I know. It doesn't seem like we should be able to."

I watch the two satellites cross paths, go their separate ways, and then disappear into opposite sides of the sky, and I'm not sure if I like being able to see them, or if it's disappointing that we've even crowded the sky with our high-speed everything. I picture the billions of texts and posts and internet searches flying across the air, bouncing off the satellites as they go, leaving glowing trails behind them until the whole night sky is an impenetrable web of wasted time.

"It's kind of sad," I say, thinking about it.

Josh turns to me. "Why?"

"Because you can't get away from all of our stuff, even out here, this far away from everything else. It's like we even ruined the sky."

"Maybe," he says after a moment. "Or, maybe it's good that you can still see it out here. Because you can see how small it really is." He pauses. "Look. All of those tiny little satellites are nothing compared to what's out there."

I sweep my eyes across the sky. He's right.

"I guess that's true," I say. And then I laugh. "You're quite the trail philosopher today."

He shrugs. "I told you. You say things out here you never would otherwise." A cool breeze rises and sweeps over us, and we both shiver.

"Should we try and zip it up?" Josh asks. "It's just gonna get colder."

I look down at both sets of our legs crammed into the sleeping bag, and the zipper that widens at our hips. "I don't think we can with both of us in here."

Josh reaches down and pulls up on the zipper, but only gains a few inches. "We're too wide like this. Here," he says as he works the sleeping bag to get the zipper on the side, "lie on top of me real quick."

I don't know what to say for a second, but then I burst out laughing.

"That's one I've never heard in real life," I say.

He laughs too. "Yeah, that came out wrong," he says,

fumbling with the zipper. "I meant so we could get this—"

"I know, I know," I say, still laughing. "Here." I lift my body and then angle it toward his until it's enough of an adjustment that the zipper finally closes us in that way. Barely.

A few seconds of silence follow, seconds in which I realize that the entire lengths of our bodies are now pressed together. I hold my head back, self-conscious of our all of a sudden very close proximity, and of my weight on him.

"I'm sorry." I try to shift so that I'm not lying right on top of him.

"It's okay," he says, his mouth so close to mine I can feel the words as he speaks them. "This is . . ."

"Nice," I finish as his stubble brushes my cheek.

Time stops for a moment and holds us there, suspended between the stars and each other's gravity. I look down at him, there in the dark, and try to fight it.

"I . . . This isn't what I came out here for," I whisper.

"Me neither," he answers back.

We lie perfectly still beneath the sparkling sky, and I can feel the cold night air, and the warmth of his skin, and our hearts beating right up against each other.

"I don't want to forget what this feels like, right now," I say.

He smiles in the dark. "Neither do I."

Our lips drift closer, and his hand slides to the small of

my back, beneath my T-shirt, sending tiny shivers up my spine. He pulls me into him, and our lips melt under the infinite sky, a million miles away from the rest of the world, in our own little universe.

UNTIL WE FIND OUR BALANCE

THE SUN PEEKS over the little patch of mountains that's visible through the trees, and I know everyone will be awake soon. My mind races, but I lie perfectly still, in the exact position I woke up in—back pressed to Josh's chest, head resting on one of his arms, with his other one wrapped securely around me. Wondering what'll happen when he wakes up.

I don't know what to do. I don't know what to say to someone I shared a sleeping bag with after a kiss that probably shouldn't have happened. I do know that it really isn't what I came out here for, and part of me feels guilty. Like I'm somehow not holding up my end of the bargain with Bri, or myself. I'm supposed to be out here to honor her, and figure myself out, not fall for the first guy I met, who happens to be sweet, and smart, and good-looking, and who saved me from being swallowed by the river.

I decide to tell him some version of this. That last night I got swept up in the stars, and being so close, and everything else. And that it was impulsive. That it won't happen again, because I need to focus on figuring things out, and it seems like maybe he does too, and I don't want to upset the balance of the group either. I hope he'll understand when I tell him that getting close to someone is not why I'm here, and the timing is all wrong, no matter how much I like him or how great that kiss was.

And then I tell myself that's all it was. One kiss. One tiny moment of connection before we fell into the kind of deep, exhausted sleep that I've only experienced out here on the trail. But now here we are. So tangled up with each other that I don't dare move.

"Mari?" Josh whispers. "You awake?"

I close my eyes, prepare my speech, and then open them again. "Yes."

"I um . . ."

Our words crisscross each other.

"I can't feel my arm," he says.

"Last night was a mistake—" I blurt.

We're both silent for a second, and then I realize my head is resting on his arm. I sit up, flustered. "Oh my god, I'm sorry." I scramble out of the sleeping bag.

Josh lies there a little bewildered and flexes his hand open and closed a few times before he sits up. His wavy hair is wild and sticks up in every direction, and the way he looks up at me almost makes me want to take it back.

"Okay," he says slowly. "I'm sorry too then? I didn't mean to—"

"You didn't—I was the one who—" I can't stop looking at him. "Anyway, let's just . . . forget about it. It shouldn't have happened, and I don't want things to be awkward."

I turn and walk back to camp before he can answer, a sinking feeling in my gut that I've just made things impossibly awkward.

At camp, I busy myself with gathering and repacking my things, which haven't completely dried yet. When I pick up Bri's journal, with its pages all puffy and warped, I miss her. I feel a little lost after last night, and even more lost without her plan for the day. I wonder what she would've written for the miles that lie ahead.

Josh keeps his distance until the others have woken up too. It's early, and aside from our customary good mornings, nobody seems to be interested in talking yet. Instead, we all set about our daily routine of filling and filtering water bottles, eating breakfast, and taping up our blisters.

No one mentions anything about last night, and Josh barely looks at me, even as we all sit in a circle for him to read from his guidebook about the portion of the trail we'll be doing today, including a two-thousand-foot climb up Bear Ridge. He reminds us that we have to make up miles from yesterday, and I feel a little sting of guilt at the mention of it. We'll have to move fast for the next two days, with few rest stops if we want to make it to our next resupply before our food runs out.

We'll be on our own to do this first section, given that we hike at different paces, but we agree to meet up at the next creek and cross it together, since it'll likely be high and difficult. I glance at Josh when he mentions this, but he doesn't meet my eyes, and now I feel even more guilty over the way I acted this morning, especially after yesterday.

There's a different energy between us all this morning. I don't know if it's because Josh isn't his usual, fearless leader self, or just that we're all tired and trying to get our heads straight for the long day ahead of us, but as we leave camp, we all sort of naturally separate and fall into our own rhythms.

I'm thankful for this. For the alone time, to think and walk. The trail drops steeply, and as I crisscross the switchbacks over the wide valley below, the panic I felt this morning when I woke starts to recede. The crunch of my boots on the dirt, and cloudless sky above, and the great swaths of trees below all center me in a way that is at once comforting and energizing. I'm surprised how quickly I find my way back into this peaceful place today, and I'm happy to stay there, outside of my mind, as I move through the changing landscape.

I don't know how many miles it is before I reach another creek, but everyone is there, leaning against rocks, sipping from their CamelBaks, and talking and laughing, and now it seems everyone is in good spirits. We get ready to cross the creek together, like we did yesterday, and I try to be casual as Josh and I link arms, because necessity trumps ego out here.

We make it without any trouble, and he gives me a quick smile when he lets go of my arm, but doesn't say anything before it's back to pace hiking. Right away, he pulls far, far ahead of me, and I can't help but think his speed has more to do with separating himself from me than getting in miles. I try not to regret what I said this morning, try to stand by it in my mind, but the farther away he gets, the more I wish he wouldn't give me so much space.

Up ahead, I see Vanessa and Jack stop for a moment, then he continues on and she hangs back waiting for me.

"Hey," she says when I get to her. "Everything okay with you and Josh? You guys both seem a little tense today."

I take a deep breath and let it out in a sigh. "Yeah. I messed up. I kissed him last night, and I shouldn't have, and now things are awkward because this morning, I told him that it was a mistake."

She doesn't say anything for a moment, and now I hope I'm not making things awkward with her too. I don't know where she stands, or what she might think of me for this. I brace myself for her to be angry or upset or judge me, but she just nods slowly.

"I figured that was coming—the two of you, I mean." She smiles. "There's definitely a little spark there."

"There is," I say. "But I don't think this is the right time or place, or . . ." I feel guilty all over again just thinking about it.

"I get what you mean," Vanessa says. "And I think he's still kind of trying to figure things out for himself after she-who-shall-not-be-named, so he probably feels the same way."

We're both quiet, and then she puts a hand on my arm.

"It'll be okay. Give it a few miles, and I bet by the time we make it to camp tonight, you guys will be fine."

"I hope so," I say. "I just want things to be like they were before. Simple."

"Then don't make them complicated," she says. "It was just a kiss." She smiles, and gives my arm a squeeze. "Truthfully, I would've kissed him too, after he pulled me out of that river."

I laugh, and so does she.

"You want me to stay back with you, or should I catch up with Jack?"

"Go ahead," I say. "I could use the solo time."

She nods. "Okay, but don't overthink it. I'll see you at the creek."

She picks up her pace, and I slow mine to let her pull away. It's nice on this part of the trail, which winds its way through lush meadows, along meandering streams before the dry, rocky switchbacks resume. I'm still behind everyone else, but I feel strong today, despite the pain in my knee from yesterday's fall in the creek. I move forward by myself, with the most confidence I've had on this trail so far. It's Bri's boots I'm wearing, but my own legs are what carry me over each mile. The daily physical punishment is familiar now, and it feels good knowing that I can handle it.

I remind myself of this as I move swiftly through more meadowland, and I try to take in the beauty all around. Today it looks like nature is showing off, and I am an impressed audience. When I see the trail begin the main climb for the day, and Josh, Beau, Colin, Jack, and Vanessa making their way up the switchbacks, I decide to give myself a moment to stop and prepare. To soak it up, like Bri would.

I slide my pack off beneath the shade of an aspen grove, sip some water, and stretch my shoulders next to the creek before I find a rock to rest on. Above me, the aspen leaves twinkle and wave in the breeze, and for a moment, I'm not here on the John Muir Trail, but right back in the meadow in front of Bri's house, looking up at the very same trees. We are young, ten at most.

"Look," she whispers. "The leaves are sparkling."

I squint up into the sunlight that streams down through the dancing leaves and smile. She's right. They do look like they're sparkling.

Bri jumps up from where we're sitting and raises her arms high above her head, wiggles her fingers, and twirls as fast as she can.

"Come on!!" she yells.

I get up and join her, and we dance and spin beneath the aspens until we're so dizzy we fall down, laughing at the way the ground tilts and shifts beneath us, until the world stops spinning and we find our balance again.

I sit watching the leaves twinkle above me now, and I look up at the switchbacks of the pass ahead, where I can see our group spread out over the trail, each person moving at their own speed, lost in their own thoughts, but all of us making our way.

Finding our balance again, with each forward step we take.

WE'VE GOT SOME COMPANY

WE MAKE CAMP at dusk, next to an unmapped stream, beneath a soft canopy of Jeffrey pines. I'm almost finished pitching my tent when I see Josh gathering water bottles to fill and filter. I grab my own and my pump, and hobble down to the water's edge to join him.

He glances up at me. Smiles. "Hey."

"Hey," I say, kneeling beside him.

It's quiet except for the sound of water over rocks, and I fumble with my pump, working up the courage to say what I replayed in my mind over the last few miles of the day's hike.

"Josh?"

I say it before I'm ready, but when he looks at me, the

words just sort of tumble out. "I didn't mean what I said this morning—about last night being a mistake." I laugh, and it sounds as nervous as I feel. "I had a lot of time to think about it today, and it wasn't. A mistake, I mean. I meant it in that moment, but then, this morning . . . I think I just . . . freaked out a little."

He nods slowly, the hint of a smile at the edges of his eyes. "I know."

"I'm sorry."

"Don't be," he says. "Last night surprised me too."

"Really?"

"Yeah." He finishes with one water bottle and reaches for another, then looks at me. "I mean, I didn't think I'd see you again after that day in the Wilderness Office, for one thing." The corner of his mouth hitches up in a smile now. "And I *definitely* didn't see us ending up in the same sleeping bag."

I laugh, thinking back to that first day we saw each other. "Me neither." Heat creeps up my cheeks as I replay last night's kiss in my mind.

He shrugs. "Sometimes things happen, so you take a chance and go with them—that's all we did. I don't think there's anything wrong with that."

"I don't either," I say after a moment.

He looks at me with those warm brown eyes, and that half smile, and I can see Vanessa was right. We're okay again. I'm about to tell him how glad I am about this, but Beau comes up behind us.

"Hey! You guys gotta come back—we got some company you're gonna wanna meet." He's smirking. "Some *true* mountain men."

Josh and I look at each other. He raises an eyebrow.

"Okaaay . . ."

"Just come on," Beau says. "You can get back to your little romantic moment after." He turns to leave before either one of us can say anything, and Josh and I gather the water bottles and follow him without acknowledging what he just said.

As we approach the campsite, I hear Colin's voice first, and after having spent the last handful of days with him, I can recognize the amused lilt in it. "So you guys just got on the trail today?" he's asking someone.

"Yeeaahh," an unfamiliar voice answers. "Joined up from Vermilion Valley Resort. *Brutal* first day, man, but that's what we're out here for, you know? For the whole experience—the good, the bad, the painful, and the transcendent."

We step up just in time to see Colin and Jack nodding in exaggerated understanding at two guys whose backs are to us. I can tell they're trying not to laugh. Vanessa's having to work at it too. I eye the wood-framed, canvas packs both of the new guys are wearing. They look more decorative than functional.

Vanessa clears her throat. "Mari . . . Josh . . . meet our new friends, Milo and Asher. They're *thru-hiking*. All the way to *Mexico*."

"Wow," I say. "That's amazing."

And it is. Amazing that they think they're going to make it to Mexico dressed like they are. I'm definitely no expert, but these guys look like they just stepped out of a hipster Instagram feed. Both look like they're in their mid-twenties, though they could be hiding younger faces behind their beards. They're dressed in flannel shirts, jeans cut off at the calves, and vintage-looking leather boots that have to be killing their feet.

Milo and Asher both extend their hands, and Josh and I take turns shaking with each one. I try not to be obvious about looking them and their gear choices over.

"Nice to meet you guys," Josh says without missing a beat. "You hiking on, or do you need a place to camp tonight? Plenty of room here if you need a place to crash."

"Thanks, man," the one with glasses says. He looks at the other one. "What say you, Ash? Call it a day?"

Asher looks at us. "Sure, long as you all don't mind."

"Not at all," Josh says. "The more the merrier. Pitch your tents wherever you can find a spot, and make yourselves at home." He smiles, and it's not ironic, or making fun of them, just genuine. It's the way he is. Friends with everyone, judge of no one. It makes me smile, and I add it to the growing list of things I like about him.

Soon enough, we find out that Milo and Asher have no tents to pitch—but they've got bedrolls and hammocks. I watch, fascinated, as they each search for a pair of trees to string their hammocks between, before going to fill their water bottles in the creek.

Milo comes back to where we're all sitting. "You mind if I get a fire started so I can get to boiling this?"

"Be my guest," Beau says with a sweeping gesture. The smirk hasn't left his face since he told us about our guests. I know what he's thinking. He wants to see if they can actually build a fire.

I kind of want to save them from trying and failing in front of him. "You can use my pump if you want," I offer. "It filters the water as it goes in so you don't have to boil it."

"Thanks," Milo says, "but we're committed to doing this the authentic way, like all the mountain adventurers who came before us."

"The ones with iPhones?" Beau says, eyeing Asher as he holds a selfie stick at an angle above him. "Pics or it didn't happen, right?" He winks at Milo.

Colin clears his throat loudly and Jack bites his lip to keep from laughing.

"It's not like that," Milo says. "We're documenting it for a project."

Beau smiles. "Of course," he says. "There's no reception to post it up here anyway."

"Anyway," I say, trying to change the subject, "if you change your mind, you can use the pump."

"Thank you, kindly," Milo says with a grin and a slight drawl that I'm not sure is real. Either way, he seems nice enough.

And as it turns out, he and Asher do know how to build a fire. They get a little one going just as the sun sets, and the chill of the evening settles over us. We all sit in a circle around the fire, making our dinners of freeze-dried pasta, mac and cheese, instant mashed potatoes, and of course, Colin with his ramen. Milo and Asher take turns snapping photos of each other in the firelight, and then they go to retrieve their dinner, and I watch as they rifle through their contents before returning to the fire.

Asher sits down across from me, and I note the bag of nuts in his hand. Milo has the same. They start munching away, and I can't help but wonder if that's all they've brought. I decide that if I have any mac and cheese left, I'll offer it to them instead of automatically giving it to Beau, who is always so willing to take any leftovers that his trail name should be Are You Gonna Eat That. I drain the noodles and mix the cheese powder in. Asher eyes the pan and pops a few cashews into his mouth. He looks at me.

"There is something WAY familiar about you, and it's driving me nuts trying to figure it out. You from LA? Silver Lake, by any chance?"

I shake my head. "No. Orange County," I say, but I immediately wish I didn't. I don't want to give him any way to place me if I do look familiar.

"Oh gawd," Milo says. "Cultural wasteland. I'm so sorry."

"It's not so bad," I say. "But I like it a lot better out here."

"Man, I *swear* I know you from somewhere," Asher says, and the little gnawing edge of worry that he might actually recognize me grows into something bigger.

I shrug and look down at my mac and cheese, trying to hide my face from any more scrutiny. I don't know what I would do right now if he actually did know who I was.

"So how far are you guys headed tomorrow?" Josh asks, and I'm thankful for the change in subject.

"We were planning on making twenty, but we'll see. We did six today, and I'm in the most pain I've ever been in my whole life."

We all nod, knowing the feeling.

"Best to start small and work up to the big miles," Vanessa says.

Asher smacks his thigh. "I know! I know where I know you from," he says, looking directly at me. "You're that girl."

My heart almost stops right there.

"What girl?" Vanessa asks, looking at me.

I give her one of those I-have-no-idea shrugs and try to keep my breathing even as my chest tightens.

Asher glances at her then looks back at me. "That Instagram girl who made that video that went viral—about quitting the internet and everything?"

I shake my head. "I don't know who . . ."

I don't know who that girl is anymore.

He looks around the circle to see if anyone else knows what he's talking about, and I'm relieved to see a circle of blank faces. But then Milo's lights up. "Holy shit, you *do* look like her. Yeah, yeah—the one who went on about social media, and how it's all fake, and torched her sponsors to go off and try to find something real? That's not you?"

I shake my head again. "No . . . I don't . . ."

I don't want her here. Not now.

"Man, that's trippy how much you look like her," Asher says. "Too bad. Would've been cool if you *were* her, and you were actually out here, doing this."

"Maybe," I say. I've lost my appetite, and I feel tired all of a sudden. I yawn. Stretch. Make a show of it. "Hey, you guys, I think I'm gonna turn in early." I hold out my macaroni. "Anyone want the rest?"

"Sure," Beau says, grabbing the pan before anyone else can.

"You okay?" Vanessa asks.

"Yeah, fine. I just . . . I'm tired is all."

Josh looks at me like he knows something's up. "Want me to walk you to your tent?"

I shake my head. "I'll be okay." I look at Asher and Milo. "It was nice meeting you guys," I say before giving a wave to the circle around the fire. "I'll see everyone in the morning."

"Watch out for bears!" Beau calls as I make my way to my tent.

I don't respond. Bears are the least of my worries right now.

"BEARRRR!"

The scream cuts through the night, and I bolt upright inside my tent. There's another scream. The sound of metal clanging together. Beams of flashlights swing wildly outside, throwing shadows all around. I switch my headlamp on, yank a trekking pole out of my pack, and unzip my tent all in one motion. I don't plan on fighting off any bears, but I don't want one to come plowing through my tent either. Plus, there's safety in numbers.

I jog over to where the fire was, and where everyone else is standing in various states of undress, making as much noise as possible in the light of their flashlights. I shine my headlamp in the same direction, just in time to see two large, furry behinds waddle casually back into the shadows of the trees.

"And don't come back!" Beau yells.

He and Colin stand there at the edge of the trees, cooking pans in their hands, wearing only their underwear and headlamps, and despite the adrenaline pounding in my chest, it might be the funniest thing I've ever seen.

"You tell 'em," Vanessa says, laughing. Jack is doubled over, clutching his stomach, cracking up.

Milo and Asher stand clinging to each other amid what looks like the remains of one of their rucksacks, visibly shaken.

Josh, who is also in his underwear, scans the group, and when his eyes meet mine, I bite my lip to keep from smiling.

"Everyone okay?" he asks, not looking the least bit self-conscious about standing there mostly undressed.

We all nod, and I try to look elsewhere.

Josh turns to Milo and Asher. "Lemme guess—no bear canister?"

Milo shakes his head.

"We hung our food up there," Asher says, pointing to the branch where the end of a rope hangs empty, swaying the slightest bit in the breeze.

Josh shakes his head. "They're too smart for that these days. Which is why we all use the canisters now."

"Noted," Milo says, looking more than a little chagrined. He and Asher kneel and start gathering what's left of their food bags.

"Well, that was exciting," Beau says. "But we got a long day tomorrow, and I'm freezing my ass off out here."

Colin puts a hand on his shoulder. "Let's go warm you up, buddy."

Beau drapes his arm around Colin, and they walk back to their tents together like that.

"You guys need help with that stuff?" Jack asks Milo and Asher.

"Nah, thanks man," Asher says.

Milo picks up a mangled baggie. "We're really sorry about this, you guys."

"It's all right," Vanessa says. "Just glad everyone's okay."

Jack wraps his arm around her shoulders, and they make their way back to their tent, leaving Josh and me with Milo and Asher. I expect him to go back to his tent too, especially because he's only wearing underwear, and in the light of my headlamp, I can see the goose bumps on his arms and shoulders, but he walks over to where they are and starts to help them clean up. I decide to do the same.

"That's gonna give me nightmares for the rest of my life," Milo says, picking up a half-eaten apple.

Asher shakes. "The big one came so close to my hammock, his fur brushed my face."

I look at their hammocks hanging in the shadow of the trees. I wouldn't want to try to sleep in them after that. Josh is eyeing them too, maybe thinking the same thing. We glance at each other, and I can see a question in his expression.

I answer it with my own. "Maybe you should sleep in my tent for the night, and they can have yours?"

"Oh. Um. *Really?*" Josh says, looking pleasantly surprised. "Yeah, that'll work." He looks down, finally seeming to realize he's in his underwear. "Lemme just get—my stuff." He glances at Milo and Asher, who both look beyond relieved. "And then it's yours for the night—does that work?"

"Yes, it does, brother. Thank you," Milo says.

"And you're sure you're okay with that?" Josh asks, looking at me.

I smile. "I am."

So we end up spending the night together a second time. And though we keep to our own sleeping bags, Josh reaches his hand out to mine in the dark without saying a word, and I take it, and we hold on until we fall asleep.

And tonight, there's nothing complicated about it.

LEAN IN

NO ONE IS shocked the next morning when Milo and Asher tell us with great regret, and even greater ceremony, that they're going to have to leave the trail since they lost all of their food, and that they might not even be coming back. They thank us for our hospitality, and we wish them the best of luck, and then they pack up their hammocks, have me take one last picture of them looking out over the lake sunrise, and they're gone.

I'm relieved. It was a close call, being recognized like that. And though those parts of my life and past feel almost too distant to be real, they're the absolute last things I want my little trail family to know about. Especially now.

We joke and laugh about the hiking hipsters as we break

camp, and by the time we leave, we're all in good spirits. We have a long day ahead of us, but at the end of it is the carrot that is Muir Trail Ranch. I know from Bri's letter that there will be a resupply bucket waiting there, along with real food, and even a natural hot spring bath, which I plan on taking full advantage of. I hope there's another letter too. I miss her words.

We descend into the aptly named Bear Canyon as a group, and follow the trail as it skirts along the creek. There are a few places we have to cross, but thankfully the logs placed for doing so are still usable, even with the high water level.

By the third crossing, I've started to lag behind the group, which seems to happen no matter how hard I try to keep up, so Vanessa waits for me at the end of the log, and offers her hand for balance when I step off.

"I found something I think you might like," she says with a smile.

"What?"

She holds out her other hand, and in it is a handful of tiny blueberries.

"Are they safe to eat?"

"Yeah," she says. "They're wild blueberries. The guidebook even talks about them growing around here. Look. They're all over." She points to the thick plants at the bank of the creek, and as soon as I look, the little berries come into focus.

"Wow," I say. "That's so cool that they just grow out here like this."

I walk down to the edge of the creek where I can see a cluster of them, and I pluck a perfectly round blueberry from the vine and pop it straight into my mouth. The little burst of tart freshness is the best thing I've tasted in days, and I happily pick a few more, savoring them one at a time.

"My cousin would've loved this," I say to Vanessa. And then I stop myself, not sure if I should've brought Bri up. We're having such a good time, I don't want to drag it down in any way.

"Was she a big fan of blueberries?" Vanessa asks. She tosses one into her mouth and smiles, and I realize maybe it's okay with her by now to talk like this.

I think about her question, and feel a twinge of sadness that I don't know the answer. I shake my head. "I don't actually know. But she definitely would've been a fan of this spot right here." I look around at the thick green of the trees and vines lining the creek, and I can almost see Bri standing here next to me, taking it in. I smile.

"When we were little, we used to go off adventuring in the woods and pretend we were lost and had to survive on our own. My aunt would pack us picnic lunches, but we'd try to eat the pine nuts we'd pull out of pinecones instead, just to see if we could do it." I picture us there, grimacing and spitting out the bitter nuts, and it makes me laugh.

"Blueberries would've been a jackpot then," Vanessa says.

I look down at the ones in my palm. "Yeah, they would've been."

We're quiet, listening to the bubbling of the creek beside us, and I search for something to say, some way to change the subject before it veers off into sadder territory.

"I bet she'd be really proud of you for doing this," Vanessa says. "For being out here—taking it on by yourself. That's huge. There's not many people who would do that."

"I'm not by myself anymore," I say. I look at her. "And I'm really thankful for that. For you guys, and the way you let me join the group."

Vanessa laughs. "We didn't *let* you, you just fit. That's how it works out here."

"Well, thank you. Either way."

"Things okay with Josh?"

"Yeah," I say. "You were right about that whole thing kind of fixing itself."

"Good. I'm glad." She smiles. "Should we pick some of these blueberries for the boys?"

I nod, and then dig in the pocket of my pack for something to put them in.

We spend the next half hour quietly picking blueberries beside the stream. It's peaceful and easy to be here with Vanessa like this, and it's hard to explain, but when I glance over at her and she smiles, I know this will be one of my best memories from this whole thing.

We catch up with the rest of the group at the top of Selden Pass, where they've stopped to wait for us, and to take in the view.

Josh smiles. "It's about time. We've been waiting for you guys."

"For what?" Vanessa asks.

Jack comes up to her and wraps his arm around her shoulder. "To celebrate."

"What are we celebrating?" she asks as she leans into him and smiles.

"A very important milestone," Colin says.

Beau chimes in. "Has to do with how many miles we've hiked . . . It's kind of a big deal . . ."

Josh takes a step toward me, gestures to the valley below, then looks right at me. A smile lights up his eyes. "Do you know how far we've come?"

I stopped keeping track when I lost Bri's journal, but I

try to go back to the last time I knew and estimate.

"I don't know," I say. "How far?"

"One hundred miles," Josh says. And then he smiles at me, speaks a touch softer. "We've hiked a hundred miles, Mari."

"Really?" I feel like I want to laugh or cry or both. I sweep my eyes over the dry craggy rocks of the mountains all around, and the sapphire blue patchwork of lakes nestled far below, and it's another one of those moments I know I will always remember. Standing right here on top of this mountain, with these people, feeling truly happy inside. And proud—of myself—for the first time in forever.

I wipe at my eyes behind my sunglasses. "This is amazing. I never thought I'd be here," I say, and I don't just mean the miles. It's everything else too.

"All right. Everybody squeeze. We gotta get a picture of this," Vanessa says.

Jack produces a selfie stick, expertly fashioned from a trekking pole and duct tape, his phone on the end of it. "You guys ready?"

We all crowd together, and Jack sets the timer before he holds the stick high in the air above us. We stand smiling against a dramatic backdrop of blue sky and mountains, and when I catch a glimpse of myself, I see it. That same look of freedom and happiness that Bri had in her pictures. When

I feel everyone's arms come around each other, I lean in. To them, and this feeling, and the slowly growing idea that maybe I'm not just pretending anymore. Maybe this is who I am becoming.

SOMEONE NEW ENTIRELY

WE REACH THE oasis of Muir Trail Ranch in the late afternoon, and though it's been a long day distance-wise, I feel the best I have since I began. I've hiked over a hundred miles. And right now, each one of those miles feels earned.

We head over to the storeroom to claim our resupply buckets first, since it'll be closing soon. I wait, just like I did the last time, in line behind everyone else, trying to figure out how not to have the same conversation that I did with the woman at Red's Meadow. Beau and Colin, then Vanessa and Jack step up, give the clerk their names, then sign for their buckets and step off to the side to wait. Josh signs for his next, but once he has it, he waits at the counter.

"Your turn, Bri," he says, giving me a look.

I step up to where a friendly-looking, white-haired gentleman is waiting with a clipboard.

"Name, please?"

"Um . . . Bri Young?" I hope he doesn't notice the nerves in my voice.

"You sure about that?" he asks. Then he winks and flips through a few pages until he finds the claim check. "Here you are. Sign right here, Miss Young."

I feel a little guilty when I do, and he disappears into the storage shed to get it. I look at Josh. "That was too easy," I whisper.

He shrugs. "He doesn't have any reason not to trust that you are who you say you are way out here."

"I guess not," I say, and smile, but the guilt in my stomach twists itself a little tighter at his words.

Neither do any of you, I think.

But before I can follow that train of thought too far, the man comes back with a bright orange bucket and sets it on the ground next to me with a thud. "Here ya go, sweetie. Enjoy." The bucket is heavy when I pick it up, and I can't wait to see what's inside. I turn to go.

"Hold up right there," he says, looking at me over his glasses when I turn back around. My heart stops in my chest, and I'm sure I'm somehow caught. He knows I'm not Bri.

"We're a little short-staffed today," he says with a smile,

"so I'll be checking you into your tent cabin too."

"My what?"

He looks down at his clipboard. "Bri Young, right?"

I nod, and he flips through the pages on a different clipboard. "Yep. We have you down for this week—one night."

"Right," I say slowly, like I know what he's talking about. "One night."

I sneak a glance at Josh and the rest of the group, who all look as surprised as I am.

"Okay, good. Now. The tent cabins are down along the river there." He points. "You'll find a single and a double bed in yours. Pillows and quilts too, but you'll need your sleeping bags to keep warm. Dinner's served in the lodge over there around seven. That's where breakfast is tomorrow morning too. Store, laundry, and hot spring baths are all over that way." He smiles. "Any questions?"

I want to hug this man. "How much does it cost?" At this point, I would pay anything.

"It's already paid for," he says, and now I can hardly contain myself.

"REALLY?"

This makes him laugh. "Really." He glances over my shoulder at the rest of the group behind me. "And, if your friends are interested, we had a couple leave a day early, so there's one more tent cabin available. Between the two of 'em, you ought to all be able to fit for the night."

"We'll take it," I say without waiting for anyone else to answer, and I dig in my pack for my wallet, which feels like a strange and foreign thing to do. I pull out my stash of cash, happy to finally have a way to repay the kindness the whole crew has shown me from the very beginning. Once the bill is settled and the tent cabins are ours, we walk through the ranch with our buckets like we've just checked into a luxury hotel, ecstatic to see all it has to offer.

Turns out, it's a lot. Muir Trail Ranch is a cluster of rustic log cabin buildings that include a store fully stocked with all of the sugary, snacky goodness you can imagine, a grill with real food, a lodge with a fireplace lounge decked out with comfy furniture, books, games, internet, and, like he said, a place to do laundry. We're like kids in a candy store, oohing and aahing over comforts we once would've overlooked that now feel luxurious and indulgent.

The woman inside the lodge introduces herself. She's friendly and welcoming, and lets us know that dinner will be served in an hour or so, and that it will be "barbecue on the terrace." Just when I think it can't get any better, she reminds us that there are two natural hot baths available for a charge, but that the natural springs in the meadow are free to all to use. It's probably a friendly hint to wash up before dinner, but I don't mind at all.

I don't mind anything right now, and no one else does either. We follow her directions down the path to the river, where we find our two tent cabins, with their cute little front porches, and we stand in front of them for a moment, marveling at our good fortune.

Colin lets out a low whistle. "Look at this. Miss Badass, coming through with the luxury accommodations."

"We be sleeping in BEDS tonight," Beau says with a grin.

Vanessa comes up next to me. "Mari, this is amazing. Seriously, thank you."

"Thank YOU, guys . . . for everything out here. You have no idea how much it's meant, being part of this group." It surprises me, but I choke up a little when I say it. I shake my head, not wanting to cry in front of them. "But this wasn't me. I mean . . . I didn't book this—my cousin did when she planned the trip."

"Well, thank you to Bri then," Vanessa says. She squeezes my shoulder. "*And* to you. We get to be here tonight because of you."

"No," I say. "I never would've made it this far without all of you."

"Aww," Beau crows. "You guys are the cutest. We better bring it in for a group hug, right here." He spreads his tattooed arms wide and sweeps us all up in them, smooshing us together until we're all laughing.

"Dude," Jack says, his voice muffled by the hug. "Someone here *stinks*."

Josh backs out of the hug. "I'm pretty sure we all do."

"Time to hit the baths," Vanessa says with a smile.

After we figure out our sleeping arrangements for the night, it's decided that Vanessa and I will take advantage of the enclosed baths, and the boys will head to the springs in the meadow. Josh and I lug our resupply buckets and packs to my tent cabin, which we'll be sharing with Beau, who has already claimed the single bed with his pack.

"This place is awesome," Josh says as he sets his stuff down on the floor next to Beau's bed. He takes a step toward me and smiles. "Thank you for inviting us into your luxurious tent cabin."

I set my bucket down and let the pack slide off my shoulders, almost giddy at the immediate lightness I feel. "Thank you for helping me get through a hundred miles."

He gives me a look, then takes another step toward me so that we're standing face-to-face, close. "I don't know what you're talking about. You got yourself here."

I think of all the encouragement and help everyone has given me so far. "Not exactly," I say, looking up at him.

Josh shakes his head. "You gotta stop doing that."

"Doing what?"

"Not giving yourself enough credit for what you're doing."

I look down at the floor. "I . . ."

I want to come clean right there and tell him that I never

would've done this on my own, ever. If Bri hadn't died, if that package hadn't shown up on my doorstep, if none of those things had happened, I'd probably still be sitting at home posting perfect pictures of a fake life.

"You what?" he asks softly.

I look back up at him. "I just . . . This is my cousin's trip. She was the one who was going to do it, and who planned it, and mapped it, and—"

"And you're here now," he says. "That counts for something."

We stand there, quiet, in the middle of the cabin, and I don't know what to say, and I can feel myself start to get choked up again so it's a relief when Beau comes through the door, arms full of packaged food from the store.

"You guys—I just bought them out of all their Oreos. And there's a hiker box, where people leave stuff they don't want, and I found a whole box of Cheez-Its in there—for FREE." He stops. "Oh shit. Did I interrupt something? I can eat on the porch . . ."

"No," I say, going over to my bucket. "I was just about to get my stuff out and head over to the bath."

Josh looks at me for a long moment before he turns to Beau. "Looks like you scored. Let's see what you got."

They sit down on the twin bed and Beau spreads out the snacks. I sit down on the edge of the bed across from them and slide my bucket between my knees. Though I'm dying to see what's inside, I feel self-conscious unpacking it with them right there, so I pop the lid open and peek inside. Sure enough, there's a note on top. I slide it out and tuck it into my pocket to read when I can be alone, and then I see a fresh pair of socks and underwear and a new camp towel that are right on top of the rest of the supplies. Rolled up in the towel are two tiny bottles—shampoo and conditioner—a bar of soap that smells like apricot, and a razor. Clearly, Bri was looking forward to a bath here too.

I gather it all up, along with my cleanest change of clothes. "I'll see you guys in a little while, okay?"

"Yep," Beau says, prying open the lid of his bucket. "I got just the thing to go with this stuff," he says to Josh, but Josh is looking at me.

"Enjoy your bath," he says. "You've earned it."

I stand inside the log enclosure, marveling at the reflection of the evening light dancing on the water in front of me. This "bath" is unlike anything I've ever seen. The man-made pool, which is built to contain the hot water that naturally bubbles up through the bedrock, is the size of a large spa. It's edged in river rock, surrounded by plants that sprawl wild and green at the water's edge, before they climb the walls of the wood and stone enclosure, and creep out the "window," which is an open space that overlooks a pristine meadow. It's serene, and magical, and I look up at the sunset sky through the open roof above, and thank Bri for bringing me here.

The spring water is hot when I step in, so I sink into it slowly. Steam rises around me, disappearing as it reaches the backdrop of trees that circle the enclosure and reach high into the sunset sky. A breeze moves through the highest branches and creates a soft, faraway hush like a whisper. I slip deeper into the water and close my eyes. I can hear my own breathing. Beneath it is the steady rhythm of my heartbeat, and I sink into that, too, struck by the feeling of calm it brings. Everything in me feels different from when I began. Altered somehow, in a fundamental way, after all these miles I've traveled.

I lie there, weightless in the water, until the first star twinkles above me in the twilight sky, and when I step out of the pool, it's as someone brave, and strong, and free.

Someone new entirely.

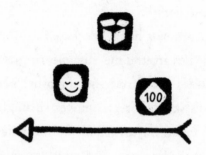

INTO THE DARK

THE TENT CABIN is empty when I get back, and I twist my wet hair up into a bun, eager to meet everyone in the lodge for dinner. I'm about to step out the door when something on my bed catches my eye.

When I walk over, I see it's a small spiral notebook. It's nothing fancy, but there's a note on top, written in messy writing I don't recognize.

Found this in the hiker box and thought you might want it to write your own hike. —Josh

I open it up and flip through the blank pages, thinking of what I might write inside, and it makes me smile—Josh makes me smile, the way he somehow knows the exact right thing to say and do. I tuck the notebook in my pack and bound out the door to tell him so.

When I reach the lodge, I can see the whole crew through the windows, sprawled out on the couches and chairs, heads down, likely checking their phones and texting their families, as we haven't had service or power since we left Red's Meadow, three days ago. My own phone and charger are in my pocket, but I'm not in a hurry to be connected again, especially because I'm sure the only things waiting for me will be calls and texts from my mom, who I still haven't spoken to since I left, and who I promise myself I'll call tonight. Later.

I take the steps two at a time, and when I reach the deck, I stop for a moment and look at the silhouettes of these people who feel like they've become my family. Vanessa sits on Jack's lap on the couch, one arm slung around his shoulders, head tipped back laughing. Josh and Colin sit on the opposite couch talking animatedly, and Beau sits holding his phone, watching something intently. He says something to the rest of the group, motions for them to come over to him, and there's a moment where they stop what they're doing and get up slowly. I watch as they gather around where he sits, and he holds the phone out in the middle, so they all can see.

And then he taps the phone, setting in motion whatever

it is he wants to show them.

For a moment, I'm sure it's some stupid, funny, Beau-type video or meme that he wants them all to watch. But then I see the way their expressions change. They go from smiling and laughing to serious, with furrowed brows. I flash back to Asher's recognition of me in front of everyone at the campfire, and my denial, and I get a sinking feeling in my stomach as I watch them watch whatever is on the screen Beau is holding.

I tell myself to stop being paranoid and self-centered. To stop making everything about me. That it's probably something funny. A dumb meme that's gone viral. Or maybe something—something big that happened in the world while we were on the trail. But the way they glance at each other, questions on their faces, makes me uneasy.

Colin pulls out his phone, and Vanessa does too, and with a tap on their screens, each of them finds something they show the others. Their phones are passed around, raising the eyebrows of each person who takes them. Vanessa hands hers to Josh, and he squints at it. "Wow," I see him say. And still, I hold out hope that they're not looking at what I think they are. That they haven't just found me out.

I step forward and take a deep breath, then I open the door, and all of their heads turn in my direction, and when

I see their faces, they look like I've caught them doing something wrong.

But really the opposite is true.

They've caught me. Pretending to be something I'm not.

I can hear my tear-choked voice still playing on Beau's phone. *"It's all so fake, and I have been too, and I can't do this anymore . . ."*

And just like the first time, it's true.

Everything I believed I was just a few minutes ago falls away, and all that's left is the sad truth of my own words. I see it in each person's face as they look at me. Pity. They feel sorry for me.

Josh takes a step toward me. "Mari—"

Vanessa stands. "I'm sorry, we shouldn't have—"

I catch a glimpse of the screen in her hand, a familiar shot of me, in a red bathing suit that leaves little to the imagination. I put a hand up to stop her. "It's okay. It's out there, you know? I put it out there."

Beau opens and closes his mouth, then stands up and takes a step toward me. "I'm sorry, Mari. I just . . . I was just killing time, and I wanted to see the girl those guys were talking about."

"Well," I say, holding my arms open. "Here I am."

It's quiet. Awkward quiet. Beau looks around.

"It's not a big deal. None of us care, right?"

Colin and Jack both shake their heads. Vanessa too. Josh just keeps looking at me with an expression I can't read.

"I, um . . ." I back up toward the door. "I think I'm gonna go for a walk."

"I'll come with you," he says, taking another step toward me.

I shake my head. "No. Thanks, but no."

He nods without saying a word, and no one else says anything either, so I walk back out the door, down the steps, and take the path back toward the tent cabin. I don't know where I want to go, other than away. Away from them, now that they've seen who I was, and away from myself too. I don't know why I thought I was anyone different out here. I've just been playing another role for a different audience, depending on them to carry me through the part.

When I reach the tent cabin, I fling the door open, go inside, and sit on the bed. I close my eyes and breathe. Try to focus on what to do. I am mortified. And so ashamed. And I don't know how they could ever trust me after this. The thought of facing them again makes me want to crawl under the covers and hide—which isn't an option either.

I glance at my pack, which is still sitting upright at the end of the bed, next to the resupply bucket. And then I'm up, scooping baggies and packages from the bucket into the pack. It's haphazard, but there's space, and I fill my pack with as much as I can from the bucket, then I close it up, cinch it tight, and pull the notebook from the outer pocket. And I write a good-bye:

Beau, Colin, Jack, Vanessa, and Josh:
Hiking with you all has been life-changing for me, and I wouldn't trade it for anything. You have no idea how much you mean to me, but I need to go it alone from here on out. I hope you can understand. Please don't come after me.
Thank you again for everything, be safe, and enjoy the last half of the hike.
Love,
Mari

I tear the page from the notebook then leave it on the bed in the same place Josh's note was left for me. And then I dig in my pack for my headlamp, heave my supply-heavy pack onto my shoulders, and walk out into the dark.

I move fast and keep my head down and my light off as I make my way through the ranch buildings, and it's not until I reach the trail junction and switch my light on that I feel like I can breathe. Which I try to do, along with telling myself that I can make it through this alone. Bri set out to do it that way, and so did I.

It takes me a moment to get my bearings, but after I sweep my light over the trail in both directions, I get oriented. And then I move. The closest I've come to hiking at night was the evening we arrived at Thousand Island Lake at dusk. This is different. There is no daylight left, and the moon is just a sliver, but I move forward through the chilled night air, and it feels right, like pushing through the darkness can somehow redeem me. Because if I can finish the hike on my own, then maybe I can earn back the right to feel good about it.

I just need to get far enough away that they won't find me if they come after me, so I push—past the noises in the bushes, and the cracks of tree branches ahead of me. Beyond the voice of reason in my head and the fear in my gut. I don't allow myself to think of all the reasons this is a bad idea. I dismiss the thoughts of predators—animal or human—as soon as they come into my head. I try not to think. I focus only on the bobbing beam of light in front of me, and following it for as long as I can, for as far as I can stand to go. And finally, when I've worked up a sweat, and am breathing hard, and it feels like I'm worlds away from anyone, I find a small clearing just off the trail. In the dark silence, I put my tent up and crawl back inside my lonely little world.

BACK ON THE MAP

I RISE BEFORE the sun, lingering for only a moment in the predawn stillness before I break camp, which consists only of packing up my tent. There are no morning jokes about the boys' hair, or team meetings about the course we'll hike today. No previews of mileage or elevation gain. No journal pages to read. I am on my own.

I sit on a rock with my breakfast of a protein bar and the last few sips of water in my water bottle, flipping through the JMT guidebook I haven't really used, looking for this section of trail, and hoping for good news—and a close water source. I pass a section about Muir Trail Ranch, then find roughly where I should be on the map and work on figuring out how my day will go. In the absence of Bri's journal—and Josh's daily summaries—this is a new responsibility for me. It makes me wish I had someone to check my plan with.

According to the guide, the trail will climb for a few miles, and then drop down through Evolution Basin, which sounds scenic and beautiful, on its way to Muir Pass, nearly fifteen miles from here. If I go by the same pattern we've been doing, reaching the top of Muir Pass is a tough, but doable goal. It's a long day, mileage and climbing-wise, but I think we've been averaging close to that, and I feel strong. Plus, I know they'll be behind me, likely pushing to reach the same goal. Which means I might actually need to go farther if I don't want them to catch me.

I finish my bar, take the last sip of water, and tuck the guidebook in the outermost pocket of my pack so it's easily accessible. And then there's nothing left to do but put my pack on and begin.

The trail starts with a traverse over open, dry land, scattered with pines and dark-colored rock. I move at a fast pace, through the still-shadowed flats, feeling a little unsettled about not having any water on me, even though I know it's only a couple of miles until I'll reach a creek where I can fill my bottle. I can't seem to focus, though. Every few minutes, I turn and look over my shoulder, half hoping, half expecting to hear the familiar voices of Josh and everyone else gaining on me.

Or anyone's voices.

The trail feels lonelier than it has since I started. And the few miles I figured it would be to get to the next creek are starting to feel long. Too long. All of a sudden, I'm worried. I stop and look around for familiar signs of water, like the green of trees I've seen lining the creeks' banks, but there are none. I strain my ears for the faraway hush of running water, but the air is still. Silent. I stand there, frozen for a moment, beneath the sun that is rising higher in the sky with each moment that passes.

And then I drop my pack and dig inside for my phone. It's dead when I pull it out. I tell myself it's fine. It probably wouldn't have done me any good out here anyway, but not having it available—even as a long shot—rattles me.

I reach for the guidebook instead.

I try to stay calm as I search the pages for the section I was looking at earlier, but all of the descriptions, and maps, and distances start to blur into something incomprehensible to me. My hands shake, and my chest tightens as I flip back and forth, just as lost in the book as I am in this moment. All of a sudden I feel hot. And thirsty.

I close the book, and my eyes, and take a deep breath. And then I take two more, and tell myself that I can figure this out. I open my eyes and look around, trying to think of what to do. If I took a wrong turn somewhere, it's fixable. All I need to do is backtrack until I find it. I haven't gone that far, it's still relatively early, and I will be fine. This is what I repeat to myself as I pop a hard candy in my mouth, turn around, and start walking in the direction I just came from.

Soon enough, I make it back to the spot where I camped, and I pause to regroup and retrace my steps from the night before. This is where it gets tricky. I stand in front of where I pitched my tent, trying to remember which direction I'd come from, but I don't know. I'd been so in my head, and in such a hurry to get away in case anyone came after me, that I'd done everything on autopilot. Again, I have to make a decision.

I remind myself that I couldn't have hiked that far last night either. So worst-case scenario, I hike a few miles now, realize it's the wrong way, then turn around and hike the other way until I get back to Muir Trail Ranch. It's not ideal, but in my head it works—as long as I didn't make more than one wrong turn in the dark last night.

But I can't think about that right now. I need to move, so I start in the direction I think I came from last night. As I go, I try to pay close attention to the landscape and make mental notes of landmarks I may need to remember and find again if it turns out I'm actually heading the wrong way—a lightning-split tree trunk, a rock pile that looks like an elephant. I focus on these things and try to stay calm and be present as I move. But almost immediately, the memory of last night, and everyone finding out the truth about me, edges its way into my mind—their faces as they watched the video, the pity in their eyes when they looked at me. All of it makes me feel even more like the fraud that I am. I've been pretending to be something I'm not this entire hike, and now I can't even run away in the right direction.

My eyes start to water, and I want to stop and sit down right there in the middle of the trail, and cry over everything I've lost—all of it because I was too scared to just be honest—about myself and my insecurities. My feelings and my fears. First, it was Bri. Then it was any sense of who I really was, or what I was doing with my life. And now, it's the group of friends that's become like family to me out here. The only thing worse than losing them is that last night, when my past came rushing back at me, I realized I'm no better off than I was when I began, over a hundred miles ago.

I still don't know what the other side of lost looks like. And right now, it doesn't seem like I'll ever find out.

A sudden rustle in the bushes up ahead brings me back to the trail in front of me. I don't see anything, but I stop immediately. Something is making its way through the tall brush, snapping twigs and rustling the branches as it goes.

Whatever it is, it sounds big. My heart knocks against my chest, and I look around frantically for a place to hide. For a second, I debate dropping my pack and making a run for it, but then it's too late.

A few yards in front of me, something tall and lean steps out of the brush. It takes a moment for me to register that it's a deer. A female. She steps onto the trail and pauses when she sees me. We look at each other for a long moment, and her dark brown eyes show no fear, just a gentle kind of curiosity. I stand perfectly still, trying to communicate to her that I mean no harm and am just passing through. A distant sound catches her attention, and her ear twitches the tiniest bit, but she doesn't look away from me. I don't know how long we stand there like that, taking each other in, but when she finally decides to move on, she disappears into the bushes without a backward glance.

I am alone again, but it feels different somehow.

I remember watching the deer gather in my aunt's meadow during the twilight hours. To her and her fruit trees, they were a nuisance. But Bri loved them. She was always sketching them, and it amazed me how easily she captured their grace and strength with just a few strokes of her pencil.

I glance at the place on the trail where the deer had stood, just a moment ago. And then I look up at the sky, blow my cousin a kiss, and thank her for what feels like a tiny nudge of encouragement.

Then I keep going.

Almost an hour later, I come to a junction and see another hiker heading in my direction.

"Hello!" he calls as he approaches. He looks about my age, has a scraggly beard and wild hair, and is wearing a backpack and the craziest pair of pants that I've ever seen— they're a patchwork of bright, mismatched fabric and look more like they belong at some sort of music festival than out here on the trail.

"Hi," I say, eyeing them.

"You like them?" he asks with a slight accent, following my eyes to his pants.

I smile. "I do. They're . . . unique. Don't think I've seen anything out here quite like them."

"Exactly, madam." He winks then extends his hand. "I'm the Fox."

I shake his hand. "Mari." I can't bring myself to say my trail name—especially being that I am decidedly not living up to it at the moment.

"Beautiful name, beautiful," he says, smiling wide. I wonder where his accent is from. Germany?

"Thank you—um . . . This is going to sound silly, but

is this the JMT? I think I might've taken a wrong turn last night or this morning, and I'm trying to find my way back."

"It's your lucky day, then, because it is indeed. The John Muir Trail. On planet Earth. Somewhere in the Universe." He spreads his arms out wide, and I can't help but smile at this happy hippie.

I breathe a sigh of relief. "Good."

"Where are you headed?" he asks.

"To Mount Whitney. I started in Yosemite."

"Ah. And I, the opposite."

"You'll love it when you get there," I say. "It's breathtaking. So beautiful."

"Mount Whitney is too, in her own way. But be careful on your own. She can be treacherous too."

His seriousness about this makes me nervous now that I know better than to go into things blindly. "Anything I should know—about that part?"

"Hm," he says. He absently strokes his beard for what seems like forever, and I wait.

"Yes," he finally says, looking right at me. "When you get to the part where you feel you're scared of going farther, just do. When you feel fear creep under your shirt and grip you from within, know that this is one of those moments from which you will rise stronger and better."

He pauses. "Welcome that moment. With open arms."

I want to ask him what he means, and what I should be

on the lookout for, but he turns to go. "Good luck to you, traveler Mari. Watch the sky today as you go. Those afternoon storms have been rolling in fast in this stretch."

"Thank you, I will."

"My pleasure," he says.

And with that, he disappears around the bend, and I am back on the map.

AND THEN I CRUMBLE

WATER. I spot the creek I was expecting to see hours ago, and I almost laugh out loud. When I reach it, I fill, filter, and drink one whole bottle, then lie back on the shore to catch my breath. After a few minutes, I sit up. Time is a luxury I don't have, and I need to make it as far as I can today, so I fill my CamelBak and an extra bottle, then get back up and begin the gradual traverse of the canyon in front of me. It's deep, the sun is high in the sky, and as I hike, I watch the light dance on the green waters that now flow far below me. Small flocks of violet-blue swallows swoop and dive over the sparkling river, and hummingbirds zip around, taking their pick from the wildflowers that bloom from every crevice available.

I push on, through meadows full of quaking aspens and pines, and continue upstream to where the trail opens up to a view of sheer canyon walls and wild waters that flow over dark ledges of volcanic rock. Next is a series of creek crossings, thankfully over footbridges and through shallow areas. There is not another soul around. It's me and the trail and the animals—for hours that stretch out, long and endless in front of me.

When I begin the steep climb up the switchbacks to Evolution Basin, I slow down significantly. I pause after the first few turns, for a breather and a drink of water, and the panoramic view in front of me grounds me in the moment. Across the canyon, streams and waterfalls flow down narrow channels so straight in the rocks, they look like they were cut with a sculptor's blade.

I wish, for a moment, I'd gotten a chance to charge my phone so I could take a picture, though I know it wouldn't do this scene justice. Instead, I try to press every detail of it into my memory—the water tumbling down over sheer rock, the endless blue sky, and the almost preternatural quiet in the middle of it all. I remind myself that *this* is what I'm here for. Beauty. Clarity. Solitude. Perspective. I tuck my water bottle back in the pack, and scan the length of trail behind me one last time for any sign of anyone else, but it's empty. So I continue on, alone.

★ ★ ★

By the time I reach Evolution Basin, I'm tired, hungry, and in need of a break after going for the last couple of hours. I find a place to stop—a good one, because it has a low, flat rock I can sit on to rest.

After I drop my pack and dig inside for lunch options and the guidebook, I sit on the sun-warmed granite, take a deep breath, and look at the view. I am sitting at the edge of a glacier-carved valley that gives way at its floor to a patchwork of alpine lakes, each shining more blue and beautiful than the next. Off in the distance, puffy clouds gather, towering above the knife-edge ridges of the mountains all around. The air is cooler up here, and I shiver despite the sun shining down on me as I scan the landscape, looking for anyone. But there is not another soul as far as I can see.

When I was with the group, we marveled at the feeling of being so isolated. But we had each other to enjoy it with. I sit there with my lunch and the guidebook, trying to appreciate this place, and that's when it dawns on me that this section of the trail is some of the most beautiful I've seen, but that also makes it the loneliest, since there's no one to share it with.

The guidebook says to leave plenty of time to wander and enjoy the five miles through the basin before you reach Muir Pass, but the late afternoon light is beginning to fade, so I pack up and prepare myself to keep going. The breeze has picked up and is becoming more consistent now. To be safe, I take the lightweight windbreaker from the pack and tie it around my waist before I head out.

The trail skirts the shore of Evolution Basin then continues up a gentle slope that lends an even better view of the basin and surrounding mountains, but it's not what's right in front of me that catches my eye, it's what I see in the distance. The clouds that were so fluffy and white before have multiplied and gotten darker. And closer. I scan the horizon, on alert for any other signs of weather—distant lightning, the far-off rumble of thunder . . . but there's nothing. Just the rush of the breeze, cool enough now to raise goose bumps on my bare legs. I put my head down and move faster, ignoring the uneasiness I feel every time I look up at the sky.

By the time I reach the outlet of Sapphire Lake, which is stunningly blue in the guidebook photos, that nagging sense of worry starts to unravel into something else. The wind kicks up whitecaps on the slate gray surface of the water. Up ahead, the sky flickers, and now I know what's coming.

I stop and drop my pack in the middle of the trail to dig out the plastic backpack cover I didn't get to use last time I got caught in the rain with Josh. I work quickly, doing my best to make sure my pack is covered with the bags, and then I put it back on and slip the poncho over my head, so it covers everything.

And then I keep going, focused on the fact that I know Muir Hut is at the top of the pass. If I can get to it, I can take shelter there, but it's a gamble that sends me headed right into the storm, on an exposed section of trail.

Lightning flashes another warning in the distance ahead.

The hairs on my arms stand in response, but I don't stop or even alter my pace. I put my head down and keep my eyes on the two-foot wide trail. Brace myself against the stiff, sudden wind that rises all around. Try to pretend that the whole sky isn't swirling itself into something dangerous right in front of me.

Thunder rumbles over the barren mountaintops, a low, angry growl that I know in my gut I should heed.

I don't.

I can't.

The only thing I can do is keep going.

Alone.

There is no one coming after me. No one following me into this storm. It hits me hard, this thought—even after all the time I've spent by myself on this trail.

It's because this is different. This feels like the night that started the whole thing.

The sky lights up again, and thunder booms in my chest, and the feeling rushes back at me so furiously it stops me right there, just as the first fat drop of rain lands on my cheek.

I look out over the jagged peaks that loom beneath the darkening sky, and wait for the feeling to pass. But it doesn't.

I am just as alone and lost and forgotten as I was that night I posted that video. And the storm that came the day after that is nothing in comparison to the one that's headed for me right now.

The wind twists, wild and angry, whipping my poncho up around me and blowing the hood off my head. There's another flash-boom, and then the sky opens up too. Prickly stars of cold rain sting my cheeks, and ears, and bare legs, and I look around, desperate for something to hide beneath, but there's nothing. I am completely exposed. My only chance is to try for the hut, which I hope is close but can't see through the downpour.

The entire sky and mountain light up electric around me, and the accompanying thunderclap is deafening. With it, the rain grows even louder and more painful, and then I realize what's happening. It's turned into tiny frozen pellets, hailstones that cover the ground, and sting my now-freezing skin.

I run.

I run with more speed and strength than I knew I had in me. Fear and adrenaline propel me uphill, through the hail, against the wind. I strain through it all, hoping to catch a glimpse of the hut, but the only thing I can see is the rocky face of the mountain and the wall of hail coming down in front of me. It puts a hard knot in my chest, and I don't have time to think. I have to keep going.

The lightning flashes again, and this time, I see something. The hut.

My chest and legs burn, but I focus on the round stone building that is now just a short distance away, and I push even harder. I close the distance as fast as my legs will carry me, and when my fingertips can reach the handle, I fling open the wooden door, and stumble over the threshold. Both knees hit the cold, stone floor with a crack, and the weight of my pack goes over my head, yanking me down to the ground.

There's a moment where I try to hold myself up, and then I crumble, right where I am.

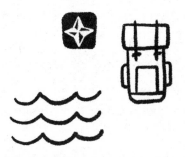

STRONG ENOUGH

I WAKE TO STILLNESS. Somewhere outside, water drips in an erratic rhythm. In the pale morning light, I can just barely make out the stones that spiral upward to create the conical ceiling above me.

For a second, it feels like I'm in a dream, but then everything comes back—getting lost yesterday, the Fox and his warning, and then the suddenness and power of the storm, and my desperate scramble up the rocks. After I'd made it inside, the storm had gotten even worse, and I'd just sat there in shock, shivering in the darkness of the stone hut, waiting for it to pass. All I could think was that I hoped Josh and everyone else had been smart enough not to try to push up the pass like I'd just done—or that they'd gotten through ahead of me.

With the storm raging outside, I'd sent up a prayer for their safety, then stripped off my wet clothes and crawled into my sleeping bag in my underwear. I lay there all night, curled in a ball, feeling foolish for putting myself in this situation, and helpless to do anything but wait it out.

And now here I am. Morning. The storm has passed.

Next to me, my pack lays open on the stone floor, its contents spilling out haphazardly after the way I'd gone through it to get to my sleeping bag last night. I grab a tank top and pull it over my head, and then I reach for the pair of shorts I'd been wearing. When I pick them up, I see something sticking out of the back pocket.

I gasp.

I can hardly believe it. A surge of hope rushes through me as I reach for Bri's letter. But the moment my fingertips feel the damp square of paper, my heart sinks. I picture the smeared pages of her journal after my fall into the river, and I almost don't want to unfold the letter. I don't know if I can handle her words being lost to me again. Especially when it would unquestionably be my fault.

I hold the letter up to the light, but the folded square doesn't give anything away, so I take a deep breath. And then I open it, as carefully as I can, and I almost cry when I see her familiar handwriting, still there.

Hey there! ≡ YOU MADE IT! ≡

Over **100** miles now, which is the farthest your own two feet have ever carried you. Be proud! Celebrate! Know that the hardest passes are still to come, but that's the point. You might doubt yourself and what you can do. But you're strong enough and brave enough to make it to the end.

And Mt. Whitney is the perfect way to finish! You'll leave the last morning, in the cold and in the dark, to a peak so much closer to the sun, to space, than you've ever been before. Further into the sky than most of the people that have ever lived have ever walked. That is an amazing thought to me. And that is what you'll do on the last day.

This hike is gonna be over before you know it now, so appreciate each moment you have left before it's time to go back and plan the next adventure. Because like Muir said,

"THE WORLD IS BIG, AND I WANT TO HAVE A GOOD LOOK AT IT BEFORE IT GETS DARK."

Love,
Bri

At the bottom of the page, there is one of her sketches. It's of a girl standing on top of a mountain, with the sun rising behind her. She holds a tiny flag with three words written on it:

A lump rises in my throat, and I hug the letter to my chest. I read it again once, twice, three times over, feeling a little less alone each time. It's hard to believe that she'd meant it for herself, but I guess she knew that even she might have her low moments out here. Either way, this letter feels like my savior at the moment, so I leave it open and lay it on the stone bench to dry completely while I come up with a plan for what to do next.

Last night, I'd been awake for what felt like all night, picturing all of the things that could be happening to my friends. This morning I want to find them—because I need to know that they're okay, and because there is so much I need to tell them. The problem is I don't know where to look. I left ahead of them, but there's a good chance they leapfrogged me while I was lost yesterday and are now ahead of me. If I leave right away, I may be able to catch up to them. This plan feels more right to me than backtracking, so I grab the guidebook to see what's coming on the next section of trail.

Every day we hiked together, we followed the same pattern: tackle the passes in the morning, descend, then make camp close to the base of the next pass. I flip through the book until I find the section that describes Muir Pass, where I am right now. Coming up is a descent, and then a long climb that includes the Golden Staircase, which the book describes as "an exposed, 1,500-foot climb up steep switchbacks." I'd be willing to bet that making it up those switchbacks is their goal for the morning, so I make it mine too. In fact, I take out the journal Josh gave me, and turn to the first page, which is blank, and I write my plan:

Catch up. Apologize.

Satisfied, I put the notebook away and pack up without bothering with breakfast. When I step out of the hut, it's not quite light yet, and I count this as an advantage. Wherever Vanessa and the boys are, they're probably still asleep.

I move swiftly and with purpose down the sandy switchbacks to where the trail skirts Helen Lake. After that, it follows a creek that drops down into a gorge lined with dark rock. In many places, the creek flows over the trail, but it's shallow enough that I plow right through. I make it through the gorge and follow the trail to where the creek spreads out into a meadow full of wildflowers, and with every step I take, I try to think of what I'll say when I catch up. Aside from saying I'm sorry, I want to tell them that they've become a kind of family to me out here. That I can already feel the miles starting to go by faster, like Bri said they would in her letter, and I want to spend this final stretch hiking with them. I want to tell them how much they matter to me. I don't know if they'll want to listen to what I have to say, or if they'll even be able to look at me the same now that they know who I was before, but I have to try.

So I keep going. Through marshy meadows and patchy forests. Over sandy flats, and dry slopes. The sun rises behind me in the sky, and morning breaks all around as I wind my way along meandering creeks that run through lodgepole forests. I focus on the trail ahead of me, searching as I go, for a glimpse of my friends through the trees. I alternate between hope and disappointment each time I come to a bend in the trail and round it only to find the other side empty. Each time it happens, I tell myself they'll be around the next one, but as the miles wear on, I have a hard time believing my own pep talk. Still, I pick up my pace. By the time I exit the long stretch of forest and see the sheer rock of the Golden Staircase in the distance ahead, I'm practically jogging.

And then I see them.

The familiar sight of their packs bumping up the trail makes me at once relieved and anxious, and I stop where I am, confronted with the reality of actually facing them. I am so embarrassed—about them finding out who I really am after I'd let them believe I was someone different, about the way I reacted when they did, about running away instead of facing it.

Bri's words come back to me then—*You might doubt yourself and what you can do. But you're strong enough, and brave enough . . .*

When I'd read that, I'd been thinking of the trail itself, and the obstacles I might come up against. But today, it's not a mountain pass or a dangerous creek crossing that I have to face, it's my friends—and myself. It's what I have to do now. Be open, and honest, and put myself and everything I need to say out there, and then hope that's enough. It's a scary thought, but on the trail I've learned to push through pain, and weather, and actual mountain ranges, so I should be able to push through my own discomfort about who I am and what got me here. That's what I tell myself as I head down the trail to meet them, and that's what I tell myself when, a few moments later, I've almost reached them.

"You guys!" I yell.

They stop. Turn around.

I wave.

"Mari!" Vanessa yells. She pushes past the boys and starts

down the trail toward me. I meet her at the bottom of a switchback, and she throws her arms around my neck.

"Oh my god, I'm so glad you're okay. We were so worried about you, especially with that storm, and then— how'd you get behind us?"

"It's a long story," I say. And then I stand back so I can look at her. "I'm glad you guys are okay too."

Josh and the rest of the guys make it down to where we're standing. They're quiet, looking down at the ground, up at the sky, anywhere but at me. I don't blame them. After what they've seen of me, I must seem like a ticking time bomb. Josh is the only one who doesn't seem uncomfortable in this moment. He looks right at me.

"I'm glad you're okay," he says.

I nod. I am. Especially now that I've found them, and have the chance to make things right.

"I'm so sorry I left," I say. "I completely overreacted back there, and it was . . ." I pause and take a deep breath. "It was because I was embarrassed. I came out here to get away from who I was back home, and when I met you all, and you were so awesome, and real, and fun, it felt like a fresh start for me. Like maybe I could be that kind of person too."

I look down at my feet then take a deep breath and force myself to bring my eyes back up to theirs.

"So when you found that video back at the ranch, I

thought it would change things, or that you'd look at me differently, or think I was a big fake, because that's what . . ." My voice cracks, and I press my lips together and breathe in through my nose to keep from crying. "That's what everyone said about me when I put that video up, and I was scared they were right—that it was true, and I was just a big joke, and I guess I . . . thought you guys were gonna think the same thing, so . . ."

I look at each of their faces, which have all softened the slightest bit. "That's why I left. And I'm sorry." I look at Vanessa now. "And I'd like to finish the hike with you guys, if you'll still have me."

It's quiet for a moment, and then she steps forward. "Of COURSE we will. That's not even a thing you have to ask—or worry about. Same with everything else. We've all done things we're not proud of, but we all get to grow and change. It's allowed."

Beau steps forward, looking like he can't keep his mouth shut any longer, and I brace myself for him to tell me what he really thinks. But he hugs me instead.

"I'm the one who's sorry, BA. I didn't mean to drag any skeletons out of your closet back there." He pauses. Looks at Josh. "This would be a good time to make your confession, since we're all laying it out there."

Josh shoots him a look.

"Confession?" I ask.

He looks at me now. "I already knew about all of that."

There's a long moment, where even the mountains seem to fall quiet.

"What?"

He shrugs. "My little sister was a fan of yours, so I knew who you were when I saw you in the Wilderness Office."

"But you never brought it up."

"Neither did you," he says simply.

"But I . . ."

"I didn't really think it mattered—except that I thought it was cool that you were actually out here doing what you said you wanted to do." He lowers his chin so we're eye to eye. "That's kinda what I've been trying to tell you this whole time."

I stand there, thumbs looped in the straps of my pack, with no idea what to do or say.

"Psst . . . ," Beau whispers, "this is the part where *you* do the whole, Oh-my-god-I-didn't-know-you-knew-that-is-so-sweet thing so we can get going again and hit the Golden Staircase before it gets too hot."

That gets everybody laughing, including me and Josh. Our eyes find each other's again, and he smiles.

"So are we good?" he asks.

I look over the faces of these people who have forgiven me more than once now, and I nod. "We're good."

"Thank god for that," Beau says. "Now let's go. My legs are cramping up."

He steps past us, and Colin follows, stopping to give me a high five. "Good to have you back, Badass."

Jack and Vanessa are next, and he pats me on the shoulder as he passes.

"Josh never said anything about it to any of us," Vanessa whispers as she passes. "Not that it would've mattered anyway." She smiles. "We all love the Mari we met out here."

"And I love you too," I say.

She takes my hand and squeezes it before she follows the others up the trail.

Which leaves just me and Josh.

I watch as the group makes it around the turn to head up the next switchback, and then I look at him. "Thank you," I say. "For keeping that secret like you did."

"It wasn't mine to tell."

"That's why it means a lot that you did."

"That's kinda what friends do," he says with a smile.

"I guess it is," I say, and I step forward and give him a hug. "Then I'm happy I have you as my friend."

His arms come around me, and he rests his chin on the top of my head. "Same."

By the time we make it to the base of the infamous Golden Staircase, the sun beats down, hot and relentless through the thin air of the high altitude. Above us towers not a staircase at all, but a series of increasingly steep, rough-hewn switchbacks that climb the almost vertical mountain wall. Josh tells us how his guidebook says it was the last section of the trail to be completed, and I can see why. I'd put this off if I could too.

But we don't. Instead, we begin, and all the way up, I think about how the things that loom large are actually smaller once you take the first few steps of dealing with them, and how Bri has been showing me this from the moment I set foot on the trail.

The climb is hot and dusty, and we stick together for this part, weaving our way, step by step, up toward the underside of the cloudless blue sky. When we finally reach the top and stand there together, I look over the faces of these people who were strangers to me not long ago, and it's almost too much, the way my heart swells when I realize that, in the miles we've traveled, they truly have become my friends.

The kind that feel like family.

LIKE MY OWN

THE NEXT FEW DAYS bring the hard territory Bri wrote about in her note. Each day holds a higher, steeper pass to climb. We rise early in the morning and prepare, mentally and physically, for the challenge of the most difficult section of trail we've covered thus far. But, like Bri also said, the rest of the hike has all been preparation for this. Strength, grit, determination. All of those qualities are at our disposal now, and they all come into play.

First is Mather Pass, a section so steep and technical that it feels more like rock climbing than hiking. The next day we tackle Pinchot Pass beneath threatening skies, and make it over just as the lightning and hail descend along-side us and we have to spend the afternoon huddled in our tents, waiting out the storm.

The day after that brings a section of trail that takes us deep into a canyon where sheer rock walls tower above us as we wade through multiple tributaries that feed the creek at the bottom. It's on this day that we have one of the scariest creek crossings of the whole trek. It happens when we reach the north bank of Woods Creek, which roars and tumbles over itself beneath an imposing suspension bridge. It sways in the wind as we all stand at the base of the metal staircase that leads up to the platform, and all I can think is that I can't believe that someone actually spent the time to build something like this, so far out here.

"So who's going first?" Colin asks.

"I will," I say. I don't know where it comes from, but I really do want to.

Jack lifts his hand for a high five, and I slap it.

"Get it, Badass!" Beau says. "Better you than me."

"And me," Josh says, eyeing the bridge.

Vanessa looks at me. "You totally got this."

I climb up the narrow staircase and stop in front of the wooden sign at the top of the platform that reads: ONE PERSON AT A TIME ON BRIDGE. And as soon as I step onto the bridge, I understand why. It dips low, then bounces back, and I have to grab the cables to steady myself.

"Holy shit," I hear Beau say behind me. "That thing is no joke."

The whole bridge sways beneath me with each step I take, and the cables groan with the movement. I look down at my boots on the weathered wood planks, and the churning whitewater far below them. And I realize something important in this moment: I don't feel like I'm wearing someone else's boots, or doing someone else's hike anymore.

This, all of it, has become my own.

We camp that night at Rae Lakes Basin, where emerald grass blooms with a prism of colorful wildflowers. We wash our tired bodies in the cold water, shivering and laughing, and feeling alive before we fall into our sleeping bags, exhausted, in the best sort of way.

Josh and I spend these nights lying together beneath the stars long after everyone else has gone to bed, not wanting to miss a moment of them, or of the time we have left together here on the trail. We talk about our childhoods and our futures, share our most embarrassing stories, and our secret hopes. It's easy to be ourselves with each other, and I can feel us growing closer in a way that I hope doesn't stop when we reach the end of the trail.

I wake early each morning, before everyone else, and take the time to write in my journal. Sometimes it's a plan for the day. Others, a note to Bri. I tell her how my time out here has changed me, and how thankful I am to her for that. I write down things I want to do when I get back—take photos, travel, spend more time with my mom, keep in touch with these friends.

I think we all can feel our time on the trail winding down, and because of that, each day goes by almost too fast. On the day we reach the summit of Forester Pass, we stand taking in the stunning view from 13,127 feet with a mix of awe and sadness. We are 199 miles into our journey of 211, and there are just two days left before Mount Whitney and the end of the trail.

The next morning, we all rise early to watch the hazy pink lift from the mountains as the sun comes up and the day unfolds, cloudless and golden, in front of us. Today, we hike at a leisurely pace, soaking it all up, because this is our last day on the trail before Mount Whitney, and because it feels bittersweet.

We reach Guitar Lake in the early afternoon, and the sun shines down through water so clear I can see all the way to the bottom of the lake. There is no one else around so we make our camp near the water's edge, then strip down for our last mountain lake swim. The water is breath-stoppingly cold when I dive in, but I take a stroke beneath the surface, seeing how far I can glide. I open my eyes, and for a brief moment, I can almost see Bri, swimming just ahead of me through the crystal water—vibrant, and full of life and joy like I know she would be if she were here now. And then she disappears.

Beneath the surface of the water, the pain of missing her is a sharp point in a still-healing wound. But when I come up for air, and I see my friends swimming in the blue of this lake, nestled in the basin of the mountains we've just climbed, beneath the endless summer sky, that pain softens around the edges into something different. Something that feels like healing.

That night, we sit around our last campfire, pooling everything we have left to eat in our packs for a trail feast. Colin cooks his best batch ever of ramen for everyone, Jack and Vanessa bring out the last of their vacuum-sealed pesto pasta—their trail specialty. Josh figures out a way to make a "cake" from a box of Betty Crocker mix he found in the hiker box, and I break out the last of my instant mashed potatoes and dried fruit. Beau, of course, supplies a little something for toasting, and we eat to our hearts' content, and sit around the fire for the last time, way past hikers' midnight, laughing together until the embers are all that's left.

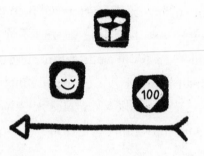

SO SHE DID

THE ALARM ON Josh's watch wakes me in the dark. He hits the button before anyone else stirs, and rolls onto his side so he's facing me. "Today's the day," he whispers. "You ready for the summit at sunrise?"

I'd showed him Bri's last letter, so we made sure to plan it out just right for us to arrive on the peak with the sun.

"Yes," I say. "No—I don't know." I nuzzle down into my sleeping bag and look up at the sea of stars. I don't want this to be over. I finally feel at home, both in the wild, and in myself, and I don't ever want to go back to not feeling that way.

"Are *you* ready?" I ask Josh.

"I think so."

We lie there side by side for a few more minutes before we wake the others, and then it's time to dress and break camp. Though there's no one else around, we are uncharacteristically quiet this morning as we get ready. We put on our headlamps and begin packing up our tents and sleeping bags without speaking. There's no need to go over the day's hike. We know that the summit of Whitney is about six miles from here—our shortest mile day of the entire trail. But in these miles is a huge elevation gain, to the highest altitude we will have reached. We eat a breakfast of Clif Bars and do one final sweep of our camp with our lights to make sure we haven't left anything behind.

And then we begin our final ascent up the rocky trail in the cold dark of night. The moon hides behind the mountains, nothing more than a faint glow illuminating their towering silhouettes against the crystal clear sky. Josh takes the lead, and this morning I walk with him instead of hanging in the back. Beau and Colin follow behind me, and Jack and Vanessa take up the rear. We move slowly, as a group, with our heads down, eyes on the ground in front of us, taking it one step at a time, as we begin the long climb.

The only sounds are of boots crunching over the dirt, and our breathing. I focus on my own breath, working to keep it calm and even as we go, because I'm already emotional. I can feel the ending that this represents, and even with all the time I've had to think out here, I'm still not sure what comes next when I have to go back to my life. I don't know what that will look like, only that it will be different from before.

"Look," Josh says. He stops for a second and points, and far below us, I can see the bobbing lights of other hikers making their way up the mountain like we are. I feel a sense of camaraderie with the people behind those lights, whoever they are. Each drawn here for their own reasons, but united by this common thing we've all decided to do. Maybe that's the point—not to have figured out life by the end of it, but to have experienced living in an entirely different way. Fully present, and in ourselves, where we have to sit with our faults and find our strengths. One step at a time.

Who knows how many steps we take, or how much time passes, but in what feels like the blink of an eye, we reach the Whitney Trail Crest Junction sign, our almost there mark. We leave our packs, taking only our water bottles as we join the trickle of hikers coming from Whitney Portal below for the final two miles. I can feel a sense of excitement rising in me now, and I think our whole group does.

We pick up our pace the slightest bit as the stars begin to fade and the sky softens into its predawn palette. Our first view of the giant, barren slope we are ascending emerges, and the trail grows rockier, the footing more uneven as it curves around to the final switchbacks. We move, up and up, and I feel in my chest how thin the air is at this altitude. Even after all of the mountains and passes we've climbed, the strain this peak puts on my body is evident in every step I take. But we are racing the rising sun, so we push back against the discomfort, and the steepness, and we keep climbing. And finally, in a moment I can hardly believe, the stone summit shack comes into view, and we've almost arrived. My legs burn and ache with the effort of each step, but knowing I'm so close gives me the energy for the final push over the uneven boulders.

And then suddenly, I've made it. I have reached the summit of Mount Whitney.

It's a surreal feeling, to be standing on top of this peak that is taller than any other mountain around, for miles and miles. I stop and take three deep breaths and try to soak up every last detail of this moment that Bri wrote about. This moment that I am standing higher in the sky than I have ever stood before, seeing a thing that most people will never see—the valley that yawns and stretches for miles far, far below us, the sun, blazing and golden as it rises in the distance, bathing the surrounding mountains in soft, rose light. The awed, smiling faces of each of my companions, glowing with the same light.

And Bri. I feel her all around me. In the sky and the mountains, the light, and the breeze that lifts stray strands of my hair and sets them dancing in the sunrise. I know she's here with me now, and that she has been all along. Every moment, every step, she's been there, helping me find my way, pushing me to find myself, and finally leading me here, now, to a place where the horizon is bright, and the possibilities are endless because I know now what's in me.

Josh looks at me and takes my hand. "And so she did," he says softly.

We watch in silence as the sun rises to its place in the morning sky and that magic, in-between moment dissolves into a new day.

Behind us, there are voices, and I turn just in time to catch the awed look on the faces of two female hikers as they make it over the crest and realize they've reached the top. When they see us, they give an excited wave, which we return, but nobody says anything. Instead, we walk the ridge slowly, with a quiet kind of reverence before we step up to the summit building to take our turns at the trail register and add our names to the long list of hikers who've come before us.

The group gestures for me to go first.

When I step up to sign it, my chest tightens, and the pen shakes in my hand as it hovers over the book. I close my eyes for a moment, then open them and take one deep breath, and then another. Tears spill down my cheeks with the third one, but I don't wipe them away.

I bring my fingers to my lips and blow one last kiss to the sky.

And then, with a steady hand, I write Bri's name.

Next to it, my own.

I look at our names there on the page, proof that we were here, that we did this together, and of one thing I know for certain—if we have the courage to make the journey, the other side of lost is a place where life, truth, and undeniable beauty are waiting to be found.

ACKNOWLEDGMENTS

I've been asked many times why I write stories about grief and loss, and in the past my answer has always been that what I'm actually writing about is life, and how beautiful and sacred it is. This still holds true for me, but there's more behind this one.

When I had the idea for this story, it was at a time when a dear family friend of ours was making her way across Europe, experiencing life and the world in a way that was incredibly inspiring to me. I wanted to weave her adventurous spirit into Mari's journey, so she became the inspiration behind Bri.

Originally, the two girls were going to do the hike together, and this would be the story of how they rediscovered each other and themselves on the trail. I loved the idea of writing about adventure, empowerment, and the bond between them. I can also remember being happy that it would be my first story that wasn't somehow tied to grief or loss.

But a few months later, this friend who had inspired me so much was in a car accident that took her life. It was a long time before I could sit down to write, and when I did, the story had changed. I wrote this book in a time when I was still deep in grief over the loss of her, but I didn't want it to be about that. I wanted it to be a celebration of all she taught me about living, and a thank-you for touching my life in such a profound way.

And so my deepest gratitude for this story goes to Sabrina Jensen. Sabrina, thank you. You touched us all with your light and joy and big fiery spirit. You taught me to be braver and more adventurous. You showed me how to live with an open heart. Still, you remind me to see beauty all around, and to cherish each day, because they are all precious. Thank you. And thank you for being with me, word by word, page by page, as I wrote this story, which I hope honors the gifts you've given me.

To Sean Jensen and Sandra Ruffini, thank you for the gift you gave all those who knew your daughter and for so graciously allowing me to weave her words into this story. It fills me with love and gratitude to see them on these pages.

To Noah Van Goa, thank you for sharing your love and your stories of Sabrina with me. I cherish them.

To my own family, thank you for being there throughout this process as you always are, with so much love and understanding, patience and support, and of course, chocolate and coffee.

And speaking of support, I couldn't make it through the writing of any book without two amazing writer friends. Morgan Matson, thank you for your title and tagline genius and your willingness to talk plot and help me find my way out of the woods. You are always the brightest spot of sunshine. And Sarah Ockler, thank you for gently being there for me as I wrote this, and for the care, insight, and sensitivity you brought to your reading of my drafts. You understand my heart in a way I am so thankful for.

A special thank-you goes to Kymba Bartley, who gave me the amazing opportunity to climb Mount Whitney in the middle of all this. Thank you for inviting me, for believing in me, and for pushing me farther and higher than I realized I could go. You are a truly inspiring woman, and I am so, so proud to call you my friend.

To my agent, Leigh Feldman, thank you for always having my back, and for your continued support, encouragement, and moxie, which I love.

To Alexandra Cooper, I can't believe it's been six books now! Thank your for helping me, once again, to find my way to the story I set out to write. I treasure your guidance and insight.

Thank you to Alyssa Miele, associate editor, for all that you do, and for making me feel like I always have someone there.

I feel incredibly fortunate to be part of the Harper family and work with an amazing group of talented people who love what they do: Rosemary Brosnan, Kathryn Silsand, Mark Rifkin, Katie Fitch, Erin Fitzsimmons, Kristen Eckhardt, Vanessa Nuttry, Bess Braswell, Audrey Diestelkamp, Olivia Russo—you are an incredible team. Thank you for your dedication and hard work. And to Annica Lydenberg, thank you for the cover art, which is so perfect for this story.

And finally, thank you to all of the readers out there. It is a generous thing to pick up a book and choose to take the journey with its characters, and it means so much to me that you do. Thank you for reading. Thank you for writing to me. Thank you for sharing your love of stories with such joy and enthusiasm. You are amazing, and I am so grateful.